C000240516

Scotland in Space

Creative Visions and Critical Reflections on Scotland's Space Futures

Editors
Deborah Scott and Simon Malpas

Scotland in Space

Creative Visions and Critical Reflections on Scotland's Space Futures

ISBN: 978-1-9993331-5-7

Published by

Shoreline of Infinity / The New Curiosity Shop

Edinburgh, Scotland

Layout and book design Copyright © 2019 The New Curiosity Shop.

Cover illustration of Astronaut Robert Burns by
Andrew Bastow

A catalogue record for this book is available from the British Library

If you enjoyed this book, find out more about what we do at

www.shorelineofinfinity.com

15-11-19

Contents

Foreword—
Steam me up, Watty

Ken MacLeod

At the original casting sessions Doohan played the character with various different accents. Star Trek creator Gene Roddenberry asked him which nationality he thought the engineer should be. Doohan replied: "All the world's best engineers have been Scottish." [1]

From coupler-flange to spindle-guide I see Thy Hand, O God – Predestination in the stride o' yon connectin'-rod. [2]

As a teenager in Greenock around about 1970, when I first saw *Star Trek* it seemed entirely natural – almost a cliché – that the engineer of the *USS Enterprise* should be Scottish. I had read enough science fiction by then to recognise genre tropes. By putting them on the small screen before a mass audience, the series fixed these tropes as canonical, indeed ecumenical: the consensus SF vision of the future. So ever since, I'd taken it for granted that the Scottish spaceship engineer was a well-worn stock figure of the genre. Perhaps he was, though I rack my brains to think of examples. It's satisfying to learn – just today – that the real reason for Doohan's fictive nationality, as of Kipling's eponymous McAndrew, was the eminence of Scottish engineers in the real world.

At the time I was discovering science fiction and studying Applied Mechanics at school, the Clyde still seemed a flourishing site of Scottish engineering. In fact it was poised on a crest, between the QE2 launch and the UCS work-in, and has hurtled downhill ever since. Today, only Ferguson Marine builds ships on the lower Clyde, and only just. Its own future hangs by a thread. Yet 'the yards' remain powerful in our imaginations, a memory of skill and industry lost and – for SF readers and writers at least – a premonition and prefiguring of a possible future. When *Intersection*, the 1995 World Science Fiction Convention, came to the SECC on the now post-industrial banks of the Clyde, the attendees' goody-bag contained a free copy of an anthology of Scottish science fiction, mostly by members of the Glasgow Science Fiction Writers' Circle, titled *Shipbuilding: New SF from Scotland*. Its cover shows a cheery female welder, free-floating above a dish aerial with a small spacecraft nearby, while a river – perhaps the Clyde – snakes away into the distance.

The imagery thrilled me then, and charms me still. It might seem a compensatory fantasy, like the heritage cranes that bristle redundant on the reach, were it not that we really are now building spaceships on the Clyde. Scotland's space industry is booming, and sites from Machrihanish to Sutherland are boosted as future spaceport sites.

Science fiction is one of the reasons why. Craig Clark MBE, founder and CEO of the satellite-building company Clyde Space, has told me that it was reading the Culture novels of Iain M. Banks that first inspired him to study the relevant disciplines and go into the business. Professor Colin McInnes MBE, who has led a succession of successful space science teams at Glasgow and Strathclyde universities, is also a long-term science fiction reader and frequent participant in science fiction conventions. Duncan Lunan has for many years combined space advocacy, literary and civic engagement in popularising astronomy and astronautics, and science fiction writing. The Satellite conventions, held every few years in Glasgow around significant space-related anniversaries, promote discussion and education in science fact as much as science fiction.

It's notable that the inspiration to do real work in space science and engineering didn't come, in Craig Clark's case, from so-called hard SF. The physics of the Culture universe are consistent, but wildly imaginary. Rigour and realism have their place: it's pinning of speculation to fact that ultimately distinguishes science fiction from fantasy. But it's not necessary to solve the equations and calculate the orbits – as Robert A. Heinlein, for instance, famously did – for speculative work to stimulate the scientific imagination and ignite the engines of enterprise. A space opera brazenly flaunting its force fields, FTL drives, improbably humanoid aliens and nested hyperspheres can set a young mind boldly going just as well.

The social sciences and the humanities might seem – to space scientists and SF fans alike – latecomers to the party, perhaps even gate-crashers, eyed as warily as hotel guests without con badges are at SF conventions. Uncomfortable memories may stir of the social adequates who mocked us nerds at school. If the contributors to this volume (and my own experience of the sociologists of science) are anything to go by, this suspicion is misplaced. The science fiction poetry of Edwin Morgan set a standard now ably continued by Russell Jones, Claire Askew, Rachel Plummer and many others [3], and has brought our peculiar preoccupations into the mainstream of Scottish literary culture. Many of Morgan's readers may be a little vague about the likelihood of intelligent life on Mercury, but so what? And the relevant social sciences – space history, space archaeology, business studies, economics, psychology – can help us see ways to make the fertile feedbacks already evident between science fiction, space exploration, and the wider society that sustains them more productive still. They show us the connecting-rods, and let us take predestination in our stride.

We can let our force shields down, and listen to what these strange humans have to say.

Notes

1. Beam up a new Scotty... from Paisley (*Scotland on Sunday*, 07 October 2007)

https://www.scotsman.com/arts-and-culture/film-and-tv/beam-up-a-new-scotty-from-paisley-1-1426291

2. Rudyard Kipling, 'McAndrew's Hymn', 1896 https://www.scottishpoetrylibrary.org.uk/poem/mcandrews-hymn/

3. See Russell Jones (ed) *Where Rockets Burn Through; Contemporary Science Fiction Poems from the UK*, 2012, and Rachel Plummer and Russell Jones (eds) *Multiverse: an international anthology of science fiction poetry*, 2018

Also: 'Steam me up, Watty' was a late-night witticism of my own, but turns out to have been the title of a 2007 event on the life of James Watt – 'one of the greatest figures in the history of Birmingham', it says here: https://www.birminghammail.co.uk/news/

Editors' Introduction

The world is entering a new era of intense activity in outer space, spurred on by political, economic, military, and scientific interests.

In the handful of months leading up to this book's publication, US President Donald Trump has made multiple proclamations about the need for a Space Force as part of the United States' Armed Forces, SpaceX has launched 60 satellites into low Earth orbit and announced plans for thousands more to create a satellite internet network with global reach, and NASA has announced it would be opening the International Space Station to private commercial use. These major headlines are all American-centric, but the United Kingdom is very much part of this global trend towards space. The negotiations for the UK to leave the European Union (*still* on-going at the time of this writing) have included a bold promise by the UK to build their own satellite system if frozen out of the EU's satellite navigation system, Galileo. And in the UK government's plans for space, Scotland is key. Scottish universities are hubs for space science and engineering. Glasgow designs and builds more small satellites than any other European city, and the Scottish space industry plans to grow its sector to £4 billion by 2030. This includes the establishment of the UK's first spaceport, from which satellites are planned to launch by the early 2020s. As the Scottish Development International website puts it, "Where once the world looked to Scotland for trains and ships, now we're famous for our satellite technology." (https://www.scotland.org/business/growth-sectors)

As Scotland reshapes itself in the eyes of the world through its relationship with outer space, now seems to be an important time for reflection and discussion about potential Scottish space identities. As a nation we are faced with questions about the ways in which we should engage with space science and technology. What principles guide our country's policies and plans for space? Where will investment for a spaceport come from, to whom will it go, and who might have to step aside? How best can we govern the satellites we build or send into space – from the location of orbits, to liability for potential collisions, to the implications of increased granularity of Earth-observations? What, indeed, is the nature of national identity when one has left the physical national-geography of the surface of the planet?

In 2017, a group of Edinburgh-based academics working in the humanities, social sciences, and natural sciences came together to form the Social Dimensions of Outer Space research network (https://sdos.ac.uk), which aims to explore these questions and many others. This group has grown quickly to include members from universities across Scotland as well as space experts, creative artists and other interested parties from outside academia. The aim of the network is to build links between disciplines that often examine similar topics from discrete perspectives, foster research projects, and work with artists, writers and publishers in Scotland to bring ideas and issues to do with space research to the public in interesting and innovative ways. We are working across disciplines to explore the ways in which greater public engagement with the scientific, cultural and social aspects of space science, exploration and industry can contribute to Scotland's space futures.

This book is one of the first productions of our network, and a result of our particular interest in the relationships between stories and space. How do the stories we tell shape the way we understand our relationship with outer space? What stories might be written about the possibilities and perils of engaging with outer space, and what narratives have guided Scotland's scientific research, technical innovation, commercial development, and public policy? Whose voices have shaped these stories, and what perspectives do they articulate? Have some perspectives been missing? Can art and fiction play roles in opening up new ideas, voices, perspectives and relationships with our own world and with others?

In 2018 we were awarded funding by the Edinburgh Futures Institute (https://efi.ed.ac.uk), created by the University of Edinburgh to find new ways of thinking about the future, to set up a project to imagine and explore possible futures for Scotland's relationship with space. We brought together a group of people that included Edinburgh-based science fiction authors, illustrators, a museum curator, and academics from a range of disciplines, including astrophysics, astrobiology, geography, English literature and science, technology and innovation studies to envisage and explore potential developments in Scottish space science. This group met at the Royal Observatory of Edinburgh, an internationally important observatory founded in 1822 during the visit of King George IV to Scotland, which has remained at the forefront of astronomical research ever since (https://www.roe.ac.uk). We held a full-day workshop, in which the project was introduced, small working groups were formed bringing a creative writer into contact with an illustrator and science, humanities and social science academics, and initial discussions and brainstorming took place. In the months after this initial meeting, each group worked together, either meeting in person or interacting through email, to prepare their materials. The literary authors wrote several drafts of their pieces, receiving feedback from their group members as well as discussing them with each other. Similarly, the academics worked on accompanying essays, receiving feedback from others in their groups when solicited. The work produced is therefore fully collaborative, and each piece is directly in communication with the others in its section, which has enabled dialogues between modes of writing and thinking that come from what are normally quite discrete disciplines.

Academics, corporations, and governmental bodies are increasingly interested in the potential connections between fiction, research, innovation, and policy. Science fiction authors are being asked to explore downstream implications of emerging technologies and to complement existing scenario planning. Our project was partly inspired by the NASA-funded book *Visions, Ventures, Escape Velocities: A Collection of Space Futures*, produced by Arizona State University's Center for Science and the Imagination (https://csi.asu.edu/books/vvev/). Their pairings of science fiction authors and academics focused on near-term technologies and "new space" – public-private partnerships and the commercialization of space exploration.

We took this model as our inspiration, and made a few changes. First, we asked our authors to start from a *place* rather than a specific technology or economic trend. As you'll see, these stories are grounded in Scotland. Visions of humanity's engagement with outer space are often discussed at the species level; we speak of the ambitions and accomplishments of a global human race. Indeed, part of what makes outer space such a generative arena for literature and law is that it provides scope for imagining who we are as a whole, and how we might govern, live, and explore together. But there are dangers in staying at the species level; a really narrow range of cultures can end up colonizing the cast of characters of 'humanity.' We wanted to write Scotland into the heart of sci-fi space futures. What stories unfold, what questions are raised about ourselves, our possible futures, and thus our present?

We also released our participants from the 'near-future' time frame and did not set specific subjects for each group beyond requiring a connection to Scotland. Our small groups were free to brainstorm together and think about space in whatever terms (wherever, whenever, even however) they wished – a freedom of which, as ought to be apparent in the range of pieces collected in this book, they made the best possible use.

From the initial brainstorming through to the submission of their pieces, we encouraged each group to converse and consult each other, sharing visions and ideas, responding to images or arguments from the other pieces in their own work, and testing the limits of their individual expertise to produce material that, while remaining intellectually rigorous, often moves beyond established academic boundaries.

The resulting collection ranges far and wide, but with strong roots in Scotland. It is split into three sections, each comprising a piece of creative writing, an original illustration, and two or three pieces of critical, social or scientific analysis that complement (and sometimes directly comment upon) the artistic work. The pieces in each section enter into dialogues about Scotland and space, projecting and interrogating potential futures, and exploring their implications for the way we live, work and interact today.

The first section opens with Pippa Goldschmidt's short story 'Welcome to Planet Alba™!', which responds to recent news about plans to open a spaceport in Scotland by imagining such a centre as a tourist attraction. Visitors can experience walking on the surface of Mars by means of virtual-reality simulation and communicate with a Chinese mission as it makes its way to land the first astronauts on the surface of that planet. This is followed by an analysis by astrobiologist Sean McMahon of the ways in which images of Mars sent back from its surface have been coloured to match the expectations of an audience for the 'red planet'; a discussion by Institute for Astronomy research fellow Alastair Bruce about the significant technical and engineering challenges that would be faced by any project to actually send a human being to Mars; and a critical discussion of 'Planet Alba™' by literary critic Elsa Bouet that places the story in a broader history of literary writing on Mars and draws out the ways in which it explores the political, technological and ecological issues examined in the other two essays.

The second section focuses both further away by discussing exoplanets and aliens, as well as closer to home with a consideration of Edinburgh as the 'Festival city' that sends its culture out to distant planets orbiting other stars. Laura Lam's story, 'A Certain Reverance,' imagines a group of artist-scientists travelling to a planet orbiting our nearest star, Proxima Centauri, to contribute to their version of the Edinburgh Festival. Coupled with this are an essay by astrophysicist Beth Biller that summarises for a lay audience the ways in which current research is able to detect, measure and determine key facts about exoplanets, and an account by Tacye Phillipson, a senior curator of science at the National Museum of Scotland, that speculates how aliens from Proxima Centauri b might go about putting together a collection of artefacts that would represent Scotland, humanity and the planet Earth.

The third section of this book opens with Russell Jones' poetic story, 'Far', in which a newly independent Scotland heads to the far side of the Universe, where it is stranded. A pair of chronotopographers – literal star-crossed lovers – seek to map the way back to each other. Astrophysicist Catherine Heymans explains how our current measurements of the Universe are only partially explained by the theory of General Relativity, why the theory of an inflation drive may be the missing key, and what this could mean for our multiverse. Matjaz Vidmar, a researcher in Science, Technology & Innovation Studies, uses maps as a metaphor to explore the production of science, stories, and the Universe itself.

Our approach has resulted in three fascinating stories that mix speculative and science fiction, and a set of accompanying essays that take a refreshingly wide variety of angles of approach to important issues prompted by Scotland's current engagements with space research, technology and exploration. We hope that this collection contributes to showing the value of speculative fiction in opening up such lines of thought. While many of the events in these stories are not anticipated to become reality in the near-term, the themes of identity, nationhood, connection to others, and relationships with and through technology are certainly relevant to Scotland today.

—*Deborah Scott and Simon Malpas*

Deborah Scott is a research fellow at the University of Edinburgh with the ERC-funded "Engineering Life" project. She's trained in human geography and law, and her research examines decision-making processes around the governance of life sciences, the environment, and outer space.

Simon Malpas lectures in English Literature at the University of Edinburgh. His research interests include studies in contemporary, Romantic and Restoration literature, the relations between literature, philosophy and science in modernity, and science fiction.

Acknowledgements

This project was developed by Drs. Deborah Scott, Simon Malpas, Fraser MacDonald, and Lawrence Dritsas. Simon worked closely with Group 1 (Welcome to Planet Alba™!) throughout the brainstorming and editorial process. Lawrence worked with Group 2 (A Certain Reverence), providing editorial guidance until near the end. Fraser worked closely with Group 3 (Far) and in the first stages of drafts; Deborah provided subsequent editorial support. Sadly, because of work and family commitments, neither Fraser nor Lawrence was able to see the project through to publication, but their work in setting things up and subsequent engagement, encouragement and enthusiasm have been genuinely helpful to everyone involved.

We were initially funded by the Edinburgh Futures Institute (EFI), in their first ever research funding, with an EFI Research Award in 2018 (https://efi.ed.ac.uk/research-awards). This covered the costs of the first meeting and allowed us to commission the professional creative writers and illustrators. A subsequent grant from EFI allowed us to work with Shoreline of Infinity (www.shorelineofinfinity.com) to publish the volume we produced. We received additional support for publication from the University of Edinburgh's School of Physics and Astronomy with a small grant from their Community and Public Engagement fund.

We want to particularly acknowledge the fine work of illustrators Andrew Bastow (Cover, Far) and Sara Julia Campbell (Welcome to Planet Alba™! and A Certain Reverence). Our thanks to Hendrik Hildebrandt and Benjamin Giblin for the KiDS dark matter maps (from the European Southern Observatory & the Kilo-Degree Survey Collaboration) and to Joachim Harnois-Déraps and Benjamin Giblin for the simulated dark matter maps (from the Scinet Light Cone Simulations) accompanying 'Far'. And our gratitude to Ken Rice, of the University of Edinburgh's Institute for Astronomy, for his enthusiastic participation in our workshop.

Our special thanks to *Shoreline of Infinity*, a member of the SDOS network and Scotland's leading science fiction and fantasy magazine and publisher, whose enthusiasm and support has been vital throughout this project. In particular, we would like to thank Noel Chidwick for his work preparing and designing this book.

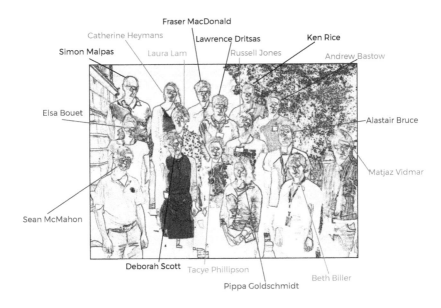

Fraser MacDonald
Catherine Heymans
Lawrence Dritsas
Ken Rice
Simon Malpas
Laura Lam
Russell Jones
Andrew Bastow
Elsa Bouet
Alastair Bruce
Matjaz Vidmar
Sean McMahon
Deborah Scott
Tacye Phillipson
Beth Biller
Pippa Goldschmidt

Andrew Bastow (cover image, Scotland at the End of the Universe) is an Edinburgh-based freelance illustrator. More of his work can be found at www.sketchheadprojects.com.

Sara J. Campbell (Scotland and Mars, Fringe in Space) is a Swiss-born Illustrator living in Scotland. She graduated from the Edinburgh College of Art Illustration course and is very interested in narrative based illustration. She worked on illustrations for magazines, packaging, books, websites and comics among other things. Sara has always been interested in science & science fiction and was brought up with Star Trek: The Original Series. More of her work can be found at www.saraljart.com

Scotland and Mars

Art: Sara J. Campbell

Pippa Goldschmidt lives in Edinburgh. She has a PhD in astronomy and she likes thinking and writing about the Universe. She's the author of the novel *The Falling Sky* and the short-story collection *The Need for Better Regulation of Outer Space*. Her work has been published in a variety of places and broadcast on Radio 4.

Welcome to Planet Alba™!

Pippa Goldschmidt

When I arrived at this place, it was a new world for me. The sun shone so much weaker than I was used to. Rocks, mountains, and a sky that was huge and so pale. I'd never been so far from home. But where was that, exactly? (An old question.) Maybe this could be home, at least for the time being.

I'd looked at it on Google Earth, of course. The first thing you do nowadays when you get offered a job the other side of the world in a place you've never visited. *What does it look like?* you ask yourself and you spy on your future home and zoom in until you hit the highest resolution; the point at which you can see offices, restaurants, cafés, apartment blocks, subway stops. Civilisation.

There was nothing like that here.

Google Earth had rendered the local vegetation in that annoying trees-as-broccoli way it had, but I doubted this place actually had many trees because it was too far north.

Actually there was a car park, looking somewhat out of place in all that emptiness. And a square building with a flat roof. That'd be the Visitor Centre, then. A kids' playground and some sort of shed obviously tucked away behind the Visitor Centre, so that it wasn't visible from the car park.

This was where I'd be living and working.

Google Earth also showed the launch pad several kilometres north, right on the coast of this country. A metal structure – presumably the gantry? – and some concrete blackened by scorch marks. It looked a fair distance away from the tourist area and there was a narrow winding road connecting the two, but no pavement or even a path. It was not somewhere you could walk to.

And nothing else at all.

I wondered if anyone had ever lived here before the Mars Project had shown up. Or if the only locals had been a flock of sheep minding their own business before the rockets arrived and barbequed them all.

That first day I'd arrived and had to look at everything, including the peculiar landscape surrounding the tourist area (so much browner and less green than I expected!), as well as all the latest and most up-to-date images of Mars in the Visitor Centre (so less red than I expected!) before I finally escaped, exhausted but too jetlagged to sleep, to a partitioned-off cubicle in the shed. The others called this shed a "portakabin", a word I'd never heard before but would hear a lot that summer. I spent some time lying on the little bed and waiting for night before it dawned (haha) on me that there *was* no night because the Sun barely set this far north in the summer, and there would be no more darkness than this greying of the light. Technically the days were only separated from each other by a sort of bureaucracy of the clock, and in fact every moment was destined to blur together with every other moment. I realised pretty soon I would have to introduce my own fake night – if nothing else than for my sanity, and so I rigged up a blanket across the portakabin window ('window'! It was a sheet of plastic) and that did the trick. Finally I slept.

The blanket went up at 11 o'clock at night and came down again at 7 o'clock the next morning. The others laughed at me but I didn't care. I slept.

I got into a routine of waking up and folding away my blanket and making my breakfast in the "kitchen" (which was a microwave, a kettle, a sink and an everlasting pile of dirty dishes), and washing in the Visitor Centre bathroom. Management were always trying to stop us doing this but they were never on site, so what the hell.

In the evening after work I would go for a walk and think about how far away I was, and what I meant by *far away* in this context, and then I would go back to the portakabin and rig up my blanket and sleep (maybe, not always).

Is there a word for a place that provides you with shelter but that isn't your home? There were plenty of times when I couldn't sleep and I would lie there watching the light eat holes through that damn blanket and trying not to listen to the others sitting around the bonfire outside, telling each other drunken stories. Or even worse trying not to listen to two of them in the cubicle next door making the whole portakabin shake so much I might as well have been in bed with them. In those times I thought about whether there was a place I could return to after this summer would be over, and did that mean that the place-I-could-return-to was the place I could call home.

The tourists area with the Visitor Centre and the car park was surrounded by – was *defined* by – its fence. I could see it was necessary to stop people sneaking in without paying, but you try living in a place surrounded by a metal fence with only one gate that shut at 6pm sharp every day (and earlier on Sundays, they took Sundays seriously here). Or maybe you already have, and don't mind. I did mind. Me and fences didn't particularly get on.

My first few days in that place I spent issuing 'Mars passports'. These were kind of gimmicky but the kids loved them. I had to stand at the entrance gate right by the sign that said 'Welcome to Planet Alba™!', and after I'd told the people driving up in their cars where they could park, I gave them the patter about leaving the Earth's jurisdiction and entering outer space where international – *cosmic* – laws applied and they therefore needed a passport. And after the more gullible tourists got somewhat perturbed because they'd left their actual passports at home, I handed them this useless bit of cardboard that was destined to end up on the floor of their car (uncharitable of me, perhaps it would survive long enough to be stuck onto the kids' bedroom wall alongside the glow-in-the-dark stars we sold in the shop).

I could tell it never occurred to any of them to think about the admin needed to set up an actual space colony. All the laws and officials and all the boring crap they'd have to do. Someone must have thought about it, somewhere. But not our tourists, and why should they? They were paying good money to escape from the dullsville of their own real lives, to come here – even if just for a day – to experience something truly out of this world!

That's what we promised them.

So, after they'd parked their cars and entered the Visitor Centre, they had to choose between the cheaper and more prosaic exhibition on Mars Science Today™, or the more expensive, and by implication more exciting, VR suite where they could experience Mars Society Tomorrow™. Or, given that they'd driven all this way, at least a hundred kilometres from the nearest half-decent hotel, and wanted to make the most of it, they usually (with only a little soft and gentle sales patter) chose the Combined Ticket allowing them to find out about Mars Today and Tomorrow™! Because that was really the best-value option for them, and spending as much time as possible inside the Visitor Centre was a chance to get out of the ever-present wind, mist and rain for a decent chunk of the day. That was what they were actually paying for – an escape from their surroundings.

The display in the Visitor Centre was most impressive and on the surface of it, quite thorough. I timed myself and it took me over two hours to read all the display boards. And yet I spotted some gaps in the information. For example, there was little mention of the first Scottish spaceport (just a brief sentence or two), although at the back of the car park I did stumble across a memorial to it, where the names of the dead were already covered over with moss that was stubborn and resisted my attempts to pick it off.

The other workers separated into individual people and acquired names. It was Tosh and Little Suze who made noises together in the next-door cubicle in the portakabin. Big Suze and McFadyan (I bet even his mother called him that) talked about datastreams and LIDAR and radar and other technical stuff I knew nothing about but I was content to sit silently and listen. 'Big' and 'Little' confused me at first because the two of them were pretty similarly sized, until Big Suze explained to me that she was a planetary geologist and interested in the formation of volcanos, mountains and canyons, and that Little Suze was an exobiologist who studied microbes and bacteria.

The others built a bonfire each night and after a couple of days in the Scottish summer the idea of something as stone-aged as trying to get warm around a pile of damp wood began to appeal to me. So I joined them outside and I'd watch them as they gazed into the flickering flames. I was good at watching locals – the people who didn't have to think about where they came from. I've always been fascinated by that sort of person.

Sometimes they asked me questions about my life, but not always, so it was generally ok.

They kept offering me their cans of beer even though I kept declining them. 'I don't drink,' I muttered each time but this upset them, especially Tosh, and they seemed to live in hope that I'd accept the next one.

As they chatted, the fire flickered in front of the distant sky which was still twilit in the north. Tosh saw me staring at it.

'Never really gets dark in midsummer,' he said. 'But just imagine being here in winter!'

'This place shuts down in winter, right?'

'Depends what you mean. The Visitor Centre does, the launch pad doesn't.'

There hadn't been any launches since I arrived and I was beginning to doubt that any rockets ever actually got launched from this place. It seemed too improbable that anyone would want to keep lugging rockets all the way up here to the top of Scotland, especially after the disaster of the first spaceport.

'The rockets get transported here by boat from Shanghai,' Tosh told me. 'Easier that way.'

I shrugged. I didn't really care.

'Where are you from, my friend?' He annoyed me with all this 'my friend' crap, he probably thought it was how I talked when I wasn't speaking English.

'Already told you, *my friend.*'

Tosh swigged from his can, but he wasn't going to give up, 'Tell me, do they have rockets in your home country?'

'Tosh, I live in the States!' and the two women laughed (as I'd guessed they would), and his question and my carefully phrased non-answer retreated safely into the landscape for another night.

After a bit I was taken off the duties at the entrance and started work in the VR suite. This was going to be my actual job here, the first days handing out passports were apparently just a test of something or other. My inability to run away, maybe.

Now I was responsible for instructing the tourists on how to get into their VR suits and headsets. We had different sizes for adults and kids, and I had to work out the most appropriate size while explaining to all the larger people that there was a reason why the suits were close-fitting, and as soon as they clambered into them and put on their headsets nobody else would see how they really looked, because in the VR world they were represented as avatars who happened to be extremely muscular and very heroic-looking astronauts.

That always reassured them. They never realised that because I wasn't wearing a headset I would be able to watch them as they walked around the room. Even as I was talking to them they kind of forgot about me, and as soon as they put on the headsets they were utterly immersed in this new world.

Once they were in their outfits and I turned on the VR display, all I had to do was watch them. You couldn't really tell one person from the other (of course you could tell the adults from the kids but that was the only distinction), they were all just people. Just humans on another planet.

And you could watch as everything fell away from them. All the annoyances about the long drive north to this place, and the bickering between the parents, and the kids mucking around in the back seat of the car and the staggering expense of the tickets to this place, they all disappeared.

It was beautiful and I loved it. I knew that if they were really there (on the real Mars and not on Mars Tomorrow™), they'd be arguing with each other about which crater to explore and how to set up camp and whose flag to fly and so on. And pretty soon it would just turn into the equivalent of one long tedious car journey.

But this – this was a fantasy and I got to experience it every day.

I soon realised that it was mainly Tosh who called Big Suze 'Big Suze', and he mainly did so when he was drinking, and so I started calling her 'Susan' to emphasise to her just how respectful I was and, by implication, how different to him. Anyway, by accident or (I'll admit it) design, the two of us often found ourselves (when the compound had closed to the outside world) in the weird little amusement park for the really small kids who couldn't cope with the VR suite and who couldn't read the signs in the exhibition. Susan would cram herself into a swing meant for these kids, and I'd push her back and forth while she hung her head right back so that all she could see was the evening sky and she laughed and shrieked. I liked doing that for her. And when I helped her out of the wooden seat afterwards, she'd still be laughing and claiming she felt dizzy and hanging onto my arm. I liked that a lot.

Of course, the reason we were busy was the launch of the first human mission to Mars. I watched it a month before I came to this place, the lift-off from Jiuquan launch site. The journey was scheduled to take seven months before the spacecraft actually landed on Mars, and human life there would truly begin. That was what brought so many tourists to our Visitor Centre, because this place had succeeded in getting one of only four non-Chinese licences to operate a tourist attraction directly connected to that mission. I didn't know how the Scottish Government had done it, but Susan told me it had something to do with Chinese students being given free tuition at the Scottish universities when, of course, the English and American ones were now off-limits to them (unless they could fork out the millions of yuan needed to get past the immigration paywall). And the Chinese and Scottish spoke different versions of English that was apparently just about intelligible to each other. Actually, according to Susan, most of the lecturers at her Uni in Edinburgh were also Chinese, and the real issue was not whether anyone could or couldn't speak English but how fluent they were in Mandarin.

Anyway. The Shenzhou spacecraft wasn't long into its journey from here to Mars but this was long enough for the media coverage to settle down into a routine – we'd already been told all about the astronauts, their backgrounds, their families, their previous jobs. So far, so boring. But the tourists loved it. Each day we'd show a 'live' datastream from the astronauts in which they'd tell us how they were getting on and the tourists would crowd around the large screen in the centre of the Visitor Centre and watch. And – even more exciting for them – they were allowed to record messages here to be transmitted up to the astronauts. McFadyan was responsible for vetting these messages (Management didn't want anything negative or critical being sent to the astronauts, which was understandable when you thought about it) and he was also responsible for overseeing the automated translation into Mandarin.

The datafeeds for the VR suite came from three rovers which had already landed on Mars some years beforehand and were busy crawling around investigating the surface in preparation for the astronauts' landing. But one day, we got an email from Management who told us that one of the rovers had stopped transmitting, and they gave us wording to update the relevant part of the exhibition.

'It jumped off the edge of a canyon,' Tosh told us around the bonfire that night.

'"Jumped"?' Little Suze raised an eyebrow, 'Isn't that a bit anthropomorphic?'

'Alright, it was pushed.'

I laughed.

'What do *you* work on at home?' Tosh was at it again with his questions.

'Oh, give it a rest, Tosh,' Susan murmured, 'you don't usually care about grown-up stuff like people's jobs.'

'I work on stars. How the light generated inside them gets transmitted to the outside world, and how it gets changed in that process,' my boring, too-technical answer did the trick, Tosh yawned and turned back to his beer. And he was on the other side of the bonfire so he couldn't see me and Susan smiling at each other.

It was Susan who showed me the gap in the fence at the back of the compound, and it was her – not me – who suggested one evening that the two of us go for a walk because there was something she wanted to show me.

I didn't know where the others were. Perhaps Tosh and Little Suze were already docked together like two compatible bits of spacecraft, and presumably McFadyan was playing some game (he was obsessed with retro stuff like Tetris). Anyway, they weren't anywhere to be seen as Susan and me carefully wriggled through the gap until we were out in the open. Behind us, the tourist area, the Visitor Centre, the car park, the kids' rides, the portakabin. In front of us, the mountains, the moors, the evening light. A peculiarly sweet smell to the air.

'The whins,' said Susan. 'They're gorse bushes,' she explained, 'they always remind me of the coconut ice that my Nana used to make.' Even though I still had no idea what she was talking about, I nodded.

We started to walk along a rough path presumably made by

other, earlier, inhabitants of this place. She didn't tell me where she was taking me, and she didn't have a map. She must have known this place well. We walked on and on and on, and the light was dimming and the insects were appalling. Great clouds of them, delighted at finding human flesh so far from the compound. We needed Tosh's cigarettes to keep them at bay, but I didn't want to say anything in case she changed her mind and turned back.

We were crossing a moor and going almost due north, and I was wondering how we hadn't reached the sea yet. Although the path was reasonably flat, it was still hard going and I was only wearing trainers. I was increasingly aware of the effort it was taking to keep up with her, but I couldn't let myself fall behind. On she walked, just in front of me (the path was too narrow for the two of us to go side by side) so I could gaze at the back of her neck which she kept slapping in an attempt to dislodge the insects. Off to the south-east was a distant wind farm, its turbines spinning slowly and catching the low sunlight so that they flashed messages across the land; I – WANT – YOU – I – WANT – YOU – I – WANT – YOU – I –

She stopped and waited for me to catch up, and then we stood side by side and looked at the view together. 'It's beautiful,' I said. I didn't mean it, of course, but I was aware this was a test of some kind and this seemed to me to be the most obvious way of passing it. Local woman shows foreign man the geographical features of her land. Foreign man praises these features. Local woman and foreign man fall in love, and live happily ever together after in a place where they can both legally emigrate to.

The view was unnerving, to be honest. I was reminded of something and it took quite a few moments of standing there before I realised what it was. It was all so blank. No people, no houses, nothing, and only the makeshift path and the distant turbines to remind us of civilisation. It wasn't a million miles from the Mars rovers' datafeeds.

'Did you grow up here?' I asked. It seemed a reasonable question, she obviously knew this place well enough to walk across a seemingly bare and featureless moor without any sort of aid.

But she frowned, 'No of course not. Nobody lives here now.' She looked cross, for some reason. 'Perhaps we'd better go back.'

'Please,' I said, 'I'm sorry.' This was probably the most honest thing I'd said since I'd arrived at this place and yet I had no idea what I was apologising for.

She smiled, another one of those secretive little smiles that only I noticed. (I knew I might be kidding myself about this, but what the hell. It could be a *holiday romance*, I thought.) I was close enough to see the distant wind turbines reflected in her lovely dark eyes.

'I can see electromagnetic radiation emitted by renewable energy devices reflected in your irises,' I said and she laughed and, finally, we kissed. Yes, we did.

On the walk back to the compound, she again led the way, 'Where *are* you from? You don't have to tell me if you don't want to.'

I brushed an insect off the back of her neck so lightly I doubt she felt my touch on her skin. 'I told you. America. DC.'

Such a long-ago journey to Washington and barely remembered now except for a single static image of clouds from the plane's window as we flew from east to west. From noon to sunrise. We were flying back in time and perhaps this meant we could start again. Through the oval window, the clouds visible far beneath us with the half-lit new day's sky behind them, reminding me that this really was the surface of a planet. Sometimes it's too easy to forget.

During the astronauts' next weekly vlog we watched them bobbing around inside their spacecraft like dumplings in simmering soup. They said they were keen to show us around their new home, and they kept using this word "home" as if they'd been practising it a lot.

We saw their sleeping cabins and their bathroom, and they described in detail how they went to the toilet. We saw them preparing and eating breakfast. (I wouldn't have been surprised if one of them had put on an apron and talked about 'doing the dishes'.) Apart from the lack of gravity it didn't look that much different from our portakabin; small and cramped, and somehow insistently and grubbily domesticated as if to make the point that all you needed to be human – *wherever* you happened to be in the Universe – was a microwave and some seriously horrible-looking food. Much like the stuff that was delivered to us from a distant and never-visited supermarket. We ate a lot of instant noodly things that summer. The astronauts didn't show us the view outside the spacecraft, perhaps they were bored of it already.

'It's just stars and that,' said Tosh. 'It's gonnae look the same as from here.' Little Suze shouted at him and told him he was a philistine, and he appealed to me, 'You know about stars, don't you, Ali McBaba? Won't they look the same?'

Yes, I told him, they'd look the same. Only the Sun would look a bit smaller and dimmer as the astronauts travelled further away from it, 'And don't ever call me Ali fucking Baba again or I'll pour all your beer down the drain.'

Tosh just laughed as if he found me really amusing.

It rained a lot and we couldn't sit in the portakabin watching crap movies every evening, so we decided to use the VR suite. By now, I was working in it most days but I'd still never put on a headset, never experienced Mars Society Tomorrow™ myself.

'VR virgin, eh? We'll soon sort that!' Tosh, of course.

'It'll be great,' Susan squeezed my arm.

McFadyan looked worried too, 'I get seasick real easy.'

'Chrissakes, you lot are about as up for it as a busload of pensioners on their way to a funeral,' Tosh was already in his suit while the rest of us were still struggling with the various zips, 'and turn off the avatar option, Ali, I don't want to see youse making pricks of yourselves in spacesuits.'

It was my job to choose the datafeed and I loaded up some footage from the Elysium quadrangle, taken quite recently from one of the rovers (but not the one that had committed rover-like suicide). We all put on the headsets, taking care to fit them to our faces so that nothing from the world outside could impinge upon our experience.

I was alone on a planet and everything was shades of red; the dust on the ground a deep rust, the sky paler and pinker. I was scared to move my head, scared of what else I would see, and I was very aware of my own too-fast breathing and the blood drumming loud in my ears. No other noise. All around, the planet waited for me to make the first move and I could tell it was wary.

'I come here in peace,' I whispered.

'Yeah, right,' said Mars, 'heard that one before.'

I knew I couldn't climb the mountains or abseil down the canyons because the rovers' exploration was limited to ground level, and if you tried to deviate from this the display simply went black. I'd warned countless tourists about this.

There was some feature that allowed information to be overlaid on the datafeed so that as well as gazing at mountains and canyons on Mars, you could simultaneously read little squares of text floating next to them. I knew this, of course, but had forgotten about it until a box appeared in front of me telling me that the long trench I could see in the far distance was one that had been observed by the Italian astronomer Schiaparelli in 1877 and that furthermore his discovery had been mistakenly assumed to be evidence for 'canals' on Mars, canals dug by intelligent aliens. The box hovered and then faded away. Wherever I looked a new box appeared. I was amazed at how much was already known about this place. Of course I knew that rovers had been coming here for decades, but still. I'd thought of it as an empty landscape, but now I realised it was already covered with words and numbers and human knowledge.

I was standing there, trying to peer through a text box about a distant volcano to the volcano itself, when I realised that the others were all standing on precisely the same spot that I was standing. I glanced around, but of course I couldn't see them. They were in my head, moving with me. We were together even though we were invisible to each other. The thought calmed me and I took a step forward. My first step on Mars, and as I moved, the environment swayed and settled down again to wait and see what I would do next.

I had to tell myself this planet was only an artefact.

Or perhaps it was me who was an artefact, who wasn't real. Perhaps the real me was outside looking at the dim sky through the rain and pushing Susan on the swing, with the planet invisible behind those rainclouds. And even when you could see it outside, the real Mars was a small dot in the night sky, surrounded by black, and so far away.

I felt a prickling of the skin on the back of my neck, someone was behind me and I turned around but of course there was nobody. Another view of distant mountains. Nearby rocky outcrops. And everything tinged red, the colour of clothing when it's been bloodied in a fight and not washed properly.

And then it got *really* weird. My vision started to focus in on something small on the ground even though I was still standing up and hadn't moved. The rover had obviously found something that had interested it, some sort of rock (I didn't know anything about geology, Earth or Martian) and had zoomed in on it.

I knew that these parts of the datafeed should have been filtered out of the tourist experience, only the space scientists were interested in close-up shots of pebbles. It must have been a glitch. But it was a bizarre experience to stand there motionless while my eyes seemed to be getting closer to the ground until it felt like my head was no more than a few centimetres from it. I felt like Alice in Wonderland when she shrinks to nothing.

I had no idea how long we'd spent on Mars. The headset blocked all noise from the suite, any chatter or computer sounds were silenced. I knew that at the end of the session the screen would simply come up with the Planet Alba™ logo, which was the invitation for people to remove their headsets and come back to Earth. I'd watched them do this so many times, their faces still registering something of the sheer and utter strangeness of what they'd seen, until this gradually fell away like water and their normal lives settled back on them.

And then I realised – this experience was just realisation after realisation – that the planet was not seeing us as humans but as machines. Whilst we were on the planet, we were embodied as the rovers which had made these observations and captured these images.

And as long as I stayed here, I would continue to be a machine. Mechanical diggers and glass lenses and a metal carapace. And caterpillar tracks – I knew the rovers had little caterpillar tracks just like the ones on military tanks, except smaller. The same sort of tanks I'd seen years ago on the other side of the fence. The tanks that I'd thrown stones at, along with all the other kids (and some of the grown-ups) in the camp.

I wrenched off the headset, but the change from gazing at a pebble on Mars to standing in a carpeted room in northern Scotland was too abrupt and I staggered and fell over. Around me the others were still standing, still rapt. I watched them, knowing they couldn't see me, and trying to concentrate on my immediate surroundings. Trying to bring myself back from memories of metal fences and tanks and military rockets lighting the night sky with fake stars. My breathing slowed. The hot and fusty room accepted me, as I found a chair and slumped on it, and changed from being a machine to a human again.

It was interesting, looking at the others. Normally, you can't watch someone else that close without them being aware and becoming self-conscious. But Susan and Little Suze and Tosh and McFadyan were on the surface of a planet millions of kilometres away from me. I sat as the four of them made tentative steps across this new world. Even after their time was up and they removed their headsets, they were too high on their experience to notice that I was already back on Earth and had been here for some time.

One evening, when Susan was giving a talk to a bus-load of Scouts, I lit out for the territory. It felt very intrepid, doing this alone. I set out on the same path that the two of us had walked that evening of our first kiss but this time, when I was about half a kilometre from the compound, I noticed an even smaller path branching off. This path was really too narrow for humans – it looked like it could have been made by the local sheep, and I imagined them treading along it in their sure-footed way.

I walked with no aim in mind. I wasn't an astronaut trying to gain a scientific knowledge of my new world. I just wanted to experience everything I could about this place. When I first arrived here I couldn't believe the lack of trees. Here you could see quite clearly the very roll and tilt of the ground itself with hardly anything to distract you. That was what Susan liked about it, she could point to all the features and tell you what they were and how they'd formed millions of years ago. She didn't seem so interested in more recent history; to her, 'recent' meant mesozoic. In some places water bubbled out of the ground and sometimes these different twists of water would join together to make a stream.

I had never lived in a place with so much obviously available water and so few people. Why, when people were fighting each other over water in other parts of the world (and when a lot of the talk about the astronauts going to Mars centred on whether they'd be able to liberate the frozen water there), didn't they come here to live? The presence of water and the absence of people was almost eerie.

I'd walked along the narrow path for about fifteen minutes when it came to an end in a little hollow which was home to a pile of stones so covered in thick green moss that they merged with the ground – this moss was the most effective camouflage I'd ever seen. The stones looked like they'd once had a reason to be there, but that reason had long been taken away from them.

I stood there for some time considering those stones. A pre-historic settlement? The remains of a sheep pen? I couldn't work it out. The place wasn't marked on the old paper map, which didn't show anything at all in this location. Neither did my phone (I couldn't get any signal on it and so it thought I was still in the compound). It was just a blank. After a bit I turned round and went back.

A few days – or rather nights – later. Everyone else is asleep when Susan and I make our way to the VR suite. I choose a datafeed, this time it's from an area called Eden but I'm not thinking of any sort of obvious symbolism, and I turn off the avatar option.

Silence. We climb out of our ordinary clothes and into our suits without looking at each other. I've suggested this as nothing more than a game, something fun to do in a place where we have to work most of the time. But that's a lie, of course.

Now we're on Mars and entering Eden, which proves to be a flat plain, its ground cracked into small squares like a planetary chessboard. It's easy to walk on this ground. Well, of course it is, we're actually walking across the shabby carpet of the VR suite. We're side by side, but we're invisible to each other. I feel her take my hand and now the two of us are walking together. Soon the discreet warning flashes up in the headset, reminding us we've reached the real-life boundary.

We stop. We turn to face each other. We can't see each other, we can only look into the distance at the mountains and the two small moons in the Martian sky. And we kiss. She pulls me closer and touches me and I can see nothing of her body as we start to make love. It's like making love to the air, to the clouds. To something with no weight, with no history. We are in Eden and loving each other.

This is how it will always be for us, I thought.

We went back there regularly, of course. There wasn't really anywhere else for us to go, I was far too inhibited to do it in the portakabin where the others were always within listening range. At least we managed to turn off the text boxes so that we didn't have to make love surrounded by geological information, although Susan admitted that that would be quite a turn-on for her. But we always made love on Mars. We could never just lie down on the dirty carpet of the VR suite, we lay down on the dust of Mars. I don't know why, we never discussed it. We didn't have to. And because we couldn't see (and never wanted the avatar option), we could use our other senses to know each other on this planet. (A few weeks later, as I sat waiting in the airport for my return flight, I walked through a mist of some nameless perfume being sprayed into the air of the duty-free shop and thought of her sweet coconut smell.)

Management sent a patch to correct the colour balance of the VR footage. There'd been complaints, apparently. Some of the tourists' feedback had said that the footage seemed washed out, the sky was faded and the landscape wasn't as red as they expected. So I ran the patch and was astonished by the results because now everything was almost cartoon-like, bright blue sky, bright red rocks. It didn't look real.

'None of it's real, is it?' Tosh said. 'You think the planet actually looks like any of the data they send us?' he sounded scornful. 'It's all made up, all tinkered with.'

'Even the astronauts?' McFadyan sounded worried.

'Especially the astronauts,' Tosh yawned, 'don't be so trusting.'

'Have you ever actually met Management?' I asked and the others shook their heads. Nobody met Management. Management were not meetable. And they had never (to our knowledge) actually been here, but they seemed to know an awful lot about what happened here. One time when Tosh took pity on a family who'd shown up on the wrong day – the day after their pre-booked tickets were valid – and he let them in anyway, we each received an email from Management saying that if this happened again, we'd have to pay for the relevant tickets out of our own wages.

Management cared about every aspect of the Visitor Centre, apart from how we actually lived in the run-down portakabin. Our lives were sort of too small for them to notice.

I was in the VR suite with Susan, and I wanted to explore our new world together. I suggested to her that we could go beyond the edge of the VR data but she said no.

'Please,' I said.

'Why do you want to?' she frowned.

'Because you shouldn't be subject to stupid rules when you're exploring a brave new world that has such people in it,' and I took her hand. I had spent so much of my life being boxed in. Padlocking the gate shut behind the last of the tourists each evening never stopped bugging me.

'But they haven't mapped the rest of the planet,' she said slowly as if I was thick, 'we don't have any information beyond the edge. It's there for a reason.'

'No it's not,' I was getting annoyed. 'Anyway, what about the gap in the fence? You're quite ok about that, aren't you?'

'That's because there's a real world beyond that!'

'There is on Mars, too.'

'No.'

I did persuade her to go to the little hollow one evening. I led her there, proud of myself for making this discovery and I thought she might be impressed with me for having found it without a map. But she didn't like it, for some reason.

'I don't want to stay here,' she whispered as I showed her the piles of mossy stones. Perhaps she was whispering because she didn't want the land itself to hear, to be marked by her words. 'It's wrong,' and maybe she was right. Seeing it through her eyes, I thought that the stones looked like a monument to entropy, a gradual surrender to a long decay. The skull of a small animal was balanced precariously on one of the stones, and this troubled me. How had it got there? Dropped by a bird of prey, or deliberately put there? I reached for her, but she shook her head.

'This place was cleared.' She was still talking in a whisper as we were walking away, so I had to lean close to her to hear what she was talking about, 'It shouldn't be so empty, there should be farms, communities. People.'

It was the very next day she told me she herself was leaving, and although I knew it was wrong I couldn't help connecting this with the mossy stones. She'd already decided to leave, she told me, it was nothing to do with that. She had only been planning to work here for a month or so, and in fact she'd stayed on longer because of me.

I didn't believe this but at least she had the decency to tell me on the equinox, that day when everyone in the world, no matter where they are, experiences the same amount of light. I was thankful that she gave me the illusion of feeling equal to her, however briefly.

'We'll always have the VR suite,' she added, and although I laughed along with her, I was secretly upset. The two of us had been in Eden, not in some fusty room in the Visitor Centre.

McFadyan was having problems with the automatic translator for the tourists' messages to the astronauts. It had been set up for English and the other major European languages (we had a surprising number of Dutch tourists, for some reason), but the only English it could recognise was a 'standard' textbook sort and many of the tourists didn't speak that. Neither did McFadyan who could be heard cursing and swearing, using words I'd never heard before now.

'What's *bawbag* mean?' I asked Tosh, and he laughed and grabbed his crotch.

Initially McFadyan simply cut out the parts of the tourists' messages that couldn't be translated, but eventually he got more inventive and started substituting other words and phrases. One day the astronauts were sent a clip of a young boy standing in the recording suite at the Visitor Centre, holding his mother's hand and saying 'The rocket's pandemonium gate will shortly be recalibrated. Please stay where you are. Do not pass go. Do not collect one hundred pounds.'

After that, he got fired.

Little Suze was offered a job at a water purification company and they wanted her to start straight away. There was one last night during which I seriously worried she and Tosh might overturn the portakabin and I had to stuff cotton wool into my ears, and then the next morning she pinched my cheek and was gone.

Tosh sat staring into his mug of coffee.

Only the two of us left now. Shit.

But when Tosh glanced up, to my horror I saw that he was crying. Tears kept slipping down his cheeks as I scrubbed at the caked-on gunk in the microwave and talked loudly about building a bonfire that evening.

'Aye,' he said finally, 'you do that, Man from Mars. You do that.'

And later, as the two of us hunkered down in front of a small sputtering pile of twigs and he swigged from his ever-present can of beer and I sipped my tea, he warmed to his theme, 'You're from the desert, right? You've got a thing about not wasting water, right?' (I was surprised he'd noticed me turning off the taps when the others were letting them gush extravagantly.) 'You're always trying to pretend you know what we're talking about when really, you haven't a clue, right?'

I nodded.

'It's obvious. You're one o' they friendly aliens,' he patted my shoulder, 'visiting Earth to be tempted by our women.'

'Something like that.'

'Something like that, aye. I hope it's been worth it. You gonnae teach me some of your alien-speak, then?'

So I taught him the Arabic words for 'night' and 'planet' and 'star' and 'love', and the next morning he was gone and I was the last one left.

I took to going to the VR suite each night and putting on the headset and stretching out on the Martian surface. It was peaceful there and I chose segments of datafeed recorded during the Martian nights, so that I couldn't see the planet itself. All I could see was darkness and the two moons moving so much faster than our own Moon, they practically whizzed around the Martian sky. If you can feel nostalgia for an experience you've never actually had, I would say that I was nostalgic for my life on Mars.

I supposed I was waiting for the astronauts to arrive, so I could welcome them. I supposed I wanted to be the first, for a change. To be the one who wasn't always a newcomer.

Alastair Bruce completed his PhD in astronomy at the University of Edinburgh in 2018. He currently works at the Royal Observatory Edinburgh, where he splits his time between researching active galaxies and working for the James Webb Space Telescope UK Public Engagement Campaign. He originally trained as an actor and is passionate about communicating all things space-related to the general public.

Mars:

There and Back Again

Alastair Bruce

Would you like to visit Mars? Me too. I wrote this guide for anyone who fancies making the trip. It will likely be something most of us only get to imagine but that's no reason your imagination can't get some of the physics right. This is meant to be a pocket guide for anyone wanting to get to (and get back from) the Red Planet, based in part on some of the most recent NASA thoughts on the matter.[1] Happy travels!

Mars I – what?

The fourth rock from the Sun. Mars is about half the diameter Earth and around 1/10th of its mass. It has a solid, rocky surface and a very thin atmosphere. On Earth, the average air pressure is around 1000 millibars but on Mars it's 6. The ancient surface is peppered by massive extinct volcanos, has been weathered by winds, eroded by long-gone water and has a ruddy-brown hue thanks to its 'rusty' rocks. Apart from our home planet, it is the most 'Earth-like' of any other solid body in the Solar System.

Mars II – why?

Why not? It's the next planet on humanity's to-do list. It's much easier to get to/from Mars than Venus but much more difficult than getting to/from the Moon. Mars' thin atmosphere is particularly

---

1   Human Exploration of Mars Design Reference Architecture 5.0 (2009): https://www.nasa.gov/pdf/373665main_NASA-SP-2009-566.pdf

annoying for spacecraft designers as it's too thin to slow your lander down, too thin for parachutes and too thick to ignore. The Moon is less massive than Mars and has no atmosphere so is relatively easy by comparison. Of course, humans haven't been back to the Moon for fifty years so when I say 'easy' I am of course being an idiot.

Mars III – where?

Mars orbits the Sun just like us but is more distant so takes longer to complete a full circuit. This means the direct-line distance been Earth and Mars varies a lot. As the Earth overtakes Mars on the inside track we're at our closest and separated by just over 3 light minutes.[2] This increases to 22 light minutes at our most distant and the average is around 12.5. In short, Mars is very far away. So far that it would be impossible to have a phone call with someone on Mars, unless you're prepared to wait between 6 and 44 minutes for the Martian's response to each of your questions. For comparison, the Moon is 1.25 light seconds away and it took astronauts nearly four days to get there. Alas, the speed of light is only for the massless. We humans and our probes travel at a far more leisurely pace. A journey to Mars would take months. Mars. Is. Very. Far. Away.

Mars IV – when?

Mariners on the globe have long made use of their knowledge of the tides and trade winds to make their journeys towards distant shores easier. For Mars, you need to wait for the orbital equivalent of the winds and tides to be just right. If they're not, your journey towards Mars becomes nigh on impossible. Every 26 months or so there is a window of opportunity where the alignment of Earth and Mars, as the pale blue dot is catching up on the pale rouge one, where the time is right to make the trek. To journey outside these

---

2　　The distance light travels in one minute is approximately 18 million kilometres. Our Sun is around 8 light minutes away. That is, on Earth we see our Sun as it was 8 minutes ago...

transfer windows would be ridiculously inefficient and the fuel requirements (and costs) of any mission attempting this would soar astronomically. Out of the last 11 transfer windows to Mars, we've flung something Mars-bound on all but one of them. The return trip from Mars to Earth has a similar optimal window to aim for. A useful analogy may be to think of a child on an active merry-go-round who is keen to make a rapid exit at the next available opportunity. Picture the panicked parent running after them but failing to keep up with the rotation of the ride. The transfer window is set by the reasonable times within which the child could make the jump; too soon or too late and the flailing arms of said parent will be out of reach.[3] In addition, Mars' orbit (and to a lesser extent Earth's) is a less-than-perfect circle so not all transfer windows are exactly alike. Remember the journey takes a long time so you have to aim at where the planet will be, not where it currently is. In the dance between orbital partners you have to throw yourself out into the void, hope your aim was true and that your partner will catch you when you get there...

Mars V – how?

Mass. Is. Everything. For every extra kilogram of useful payload you want to bring with you, you'll need some extra fuel to accelerate it up to transfer velocity. For every kilogram of extra fuel you add you'll need some more extra fuel to accelerate that extra fuel up to the required velocity and so on and so forth. Heavier rockets require bigger engines and are more expensive, so every single kilogram really does matter. If you want to send humans your payload mass will also go through the roof. Rovers don't need air, water, food or toilets and can withstand harsher environments than us bags of mostly water. For comparison the last lunar mission, Apollo 17, had

---

3   As to the child's reason for wanting to make a such rapid departure, and the lacklustre response of the merry-go-round attendant, I leave these details entirely up to you. The option of some thrusters to allow for course-corrections was also not afforded this particular youngster.

a payload mass of 48,607 kg. This included the command/service module and the lunar module for landing on and returning from the Moon's surface. This payload mass bought the three astronauts a grand total of 13 days in space. For two of the astronauts this included 3 days on the lunar surface and one day's worth of roaming on the lunar surface in their spacesuits. The remaining astronaut will have spent a total of 6 days in lunar orbit. In contrast to these lunar payloads, the most massive payload ever sent to Mars has been the Curiosity Rover as well as the associated fuel/rockets for parking it: a grand total of 3893 kg. We don't yet have a rocket capable of hurling the equivalent mass of Apollo 17 towards Mars, and won't for the foreseeable future. SpaceX's Falcon Heavy claims it can loft a 16,800 kg to Mars, and NASA's *SLS* and SpaceX's *BFR* (or variants thereupon) are yet to fly but both are hoping to more than double this. Given that Apollo 17 was optimised for only around two weeks in space, we have to learn to do more with less. Of course, we don't have to do everything with a single rocket launch. In fact, this is a key component for the current thinking on human-rated Mars missions.

Mars VI – 'the plan'

If missions to Mars were ticketed like cruise liners, the three more favourable choices available would be 'steerage', 'first class' and 'thrill-seeker'. The first two options are variants on a Mars mission type deemed Conjunction Class. This mission type would seek to use fuel-optimal transfer windows to and from Mars, which means astronauts would have an extended stay on the surface of more than 500 days waiting for the most efficient return opportunity (waiting for the Earth to catch up on the inside track again) and, including travel time, a total mission duration of 900 days. The 'thrill-seeker' package belongs to the mission type deemed Opposition Class. This mission type would make do with only one fuel-optimal transfer window and would only stay at Mars for around 30–90 days. The non-optimal transfer part of the journey would take longer and would bring the mission closer to the Sun than the planet Venus owing to the more dramatic flight path required to make up for the misalignment of Earth and Mars on this leg. You'd spend most of your 500–650-day mission in space. You might even get a gravity assist from Venus which is why I've termed this one the 'thrill-seeker'. That brief view of Venus might be worth paying for. Whichever package you opt for, it is clear that we're well beyond the two weeks needed to journey to the Moon and back.

The thinking behind current Mars planning is to fly the equipment needed to Mars well in advance of the arrival of any humans. This allows you to launch multiple rockets with the various components needed, in particular the habitation modules and return rocket. To be really efficient, this return rocket could spend time making its own rocket fuel on arrival at Mars. You would bring some hydrogen and react it with carbon dioxide from the Martian atmosphere to generate both methane and oxygen, your propellant for the return trip. The added bonus of this 'equipment first' approach is that you'd have at least until the next Earth>Mars transfer window to ensure all of it was functioning as intended before sending your humans aloft. The steerage option I mentioned above would fall to all of these cargo flights as these would only ever use the most fuel-efficient (and perhaps longer) trajectories, helping to keep the cost down. The first-class option would, for an increase in fuel cost, allow the humans to take a less optimal but quicker trajectory to Mars. This is advisable for two reasons: the first is that long-term microgravity is not good for human physiology (leading to bone loss and muscle atrophy) and the second is that interplanetary space increases radiation exposure for the crew (mainly from solar proton events and galactic cosmic rays). These are both very good reasons to minimise the journey time to and from Mars.

Mars VII – the 'to-do' list

Clearly a human-rated Mars programme will be complex and costly. If we're optimistic and assume that the financial and political commitments can be met, that leaves us thinking about the many hurdles which will need to be overcome. Many mission parameters are still in flux as new rockets and capsule hardware make it to the flight-ready stage. Here are some outstanding questions that might have a particular impact on your trip.

The right engines for the job. If you want to use methane as your return fuel then you need an engine designed to work with this propellant. Some methane rockets are in development already. Perhaps a more pressing concern is which engines are best suited to providing the kick needed to make the journey from Earth to Mars. Chemical rockets aren't the only available option and it turns out that they're pretty poor for making efficient interplanetary journeys. Every kilogram matters so other options are also being considered. One alternative is to use nuclear thermal propulsion. It sounds like sci-fi (then again, we are going to Mars) but these engines have been tested in the past and they can provide significant payload gains over chemical rockets. As per NASA's thinking in 2009, this is their currently preferred option for human flights to Mars. Nuclear power isn't just being considered for the journey but also for the stay on the Martian surface (cooking up your own rocket fuel needs a bit of juice). You'd need to be pretty comfortable living next to a fission reactor for most of your trip but they are a viable option. The other candidate for the trip is the possibility of using solar electric propulsion methods; one variant of these are ion thrusters, where electron-stripped atoms (typically Xenon gas) are expelled at very high speeds to produce thrust. Notable for their characteristic 'blue' glow they deliver a low thrust but are incredibly efficient. Currently better suited to small probes and uncrewed missions, we're some way off having enough power in these engines for human-rated missions à la 'The Martian'. However, there is a huge potential in solar electric propulsion and these engines may become viable options in the not-too-distant future. Plus, they do look cool.

Your health and well-being. What's the longest trip you've ever taken? Would you be willing to share the same space in the same capsules with the same crew for three years? Would you be willing to accept the lack of real-time contact with anyone back home? Not to mention the psychological impact of a long-duration spaceflight, you will also have to contend with an increased risk of medical trouble. Valeri Polyakov currently holds the record for a single stint in space of 438 days on the Mir space station. This is around half of what would be required for the currently favoured long-stay Mars missions. We know that prolonged exposure to microgravity results in a significant decrease in bone/muscle mass in addition to numerous other detrimental effects. These can be mitigated to a certain extent, for example via a rigorous exercise regime, but are very difficult to negate entirely. The increased radiation environment on the journey to Mars is also a worry and there is much still to learn about the radiation environment on the Martian surface. High-energy particles can come from solar events or cosmic rays and there are questions still to answer about how best to shield your mission from such effects in a way that keeps the mass of any spacecraft/habitat shielding to a minimum. The longer the trip, the greater the chance of an acute medical emergency as well. A capsule is a lousy place for your appendix to start acting up. In short, it will be no walk in the park for any Mars crew. Would you be willing to accept the increased risks?

Could we fly to Mars from Scotland? I have been asking myself this question for fun, in the hope that we win some galactic lottery and could afford to start our very own Mars programme. Scotland, at its relatively high latitude, is not always the most ideal place to launch satellites from, particularly if one is interested in getting to geostationary orbits which are equatorial. This is because any probe launching into Earth orbit from a high latitude will be inclined relative to the planet's equator by at least that amount. However, we are in a good position to launch satellites on polar orbits, which may become a reality very soon with our first dedicated spaceport(s) on the horizon. When it comes to getting to Mars there will in fact be some occasions where the desired transfer orbit inclination is high for a small number of transfer windows, meaning our high latitude would actually favour us over lower-latitude launch sites such as Cape Canaveral. On occasions when the optimal transfer inclination is low, anything launched from Scotland would need to expend extra fuel to adjust the orbital inclination of any 'McSpacecraft' before embarking on the interplanetary leg. If money were no object, this would be a relatively small price to pay. Another consideration is the direction of launch – we are surrounded by water on three sides but we would need to take care not to drop any expended rocket boosters on our Nordic cousins...

How we choose to overcome these problems so that we can first-foot our neighbour planet is going to be exciting and, I think, part of what it means to be human. I also hope we treat the natural beauty of the pale rouge one with a little more respect than the pale blue one from the off. I can't wait to see how our first foray beyond the Earth-Moon system progresses.

One last thing, don't forget your towel...

Sean McMahon is a Marie Skłodowska-Curie Fellow in the UK Centre for Astrobiology, and soon to be a Chancellor's Fellow in Astrobiology at the University of Edinburgh. Sean is a planetary geologist and palaeontologist.

The R** Planet:
what colour is Mars?

Sean McMahon

On July 21, 1976, NASA's Viking 1 Lander captured the first colour photograph to be taken on Mars (or any other planet beside Earth). The sky was coral pink; too pink for overcautious NASA technicians, who toned it down to a flat grey before publishing the image. This became bluish when reproduced, and the world's media delightedly reported the blue skies on Mars until the unfiltered originals were released. We've been confused and misled about the colour of Mars ever since. Artists and movie-makers drown their impressions of Mars in a nightmarish blood-hued marinade. Cranks on the internet claim the Martian sky really is an earthly blue that NASA has conspired to cover up.

But carefully calibrated photographs from rovers – as close as we can get to "true colour" – reveal a natural palette as rich, subtle, and surprising as the flesh tones of a Rembrandt. The sky, infused with light-scattering ferric dust, is usually milky beige, tan, or coffee-coloured, sometimes darkening to olive green or an impressive burnished gold. The small, pale sun glows blue at sunrise and sunset, and at twilight this colour sometimes reappears in streaky high-altitude clouds. Beneath a fine coating of dust, the rocks are mostly copper-brown, blue-grey, and black.

The colour of Mars is important to me. As a planetary geologist, I have looked at photographs of Mars for perhaps hundreds of hours. It is an experience that has prompted me to defend this planet against those who would re-engineer it. Although profoundly hostile to life, Mars has a quiet, still, and inviting beauty of its own, shaped over billions of years. To overlook this — to see only red — is a kind of aesthetic negligence, deeply connected (as in the novels of Kim Stanley Robinson) with the hubristic desire to remould Mars in the image of the Earth. We colourise to colonise.

The images on the following page were produced by reducing approximate-true-colour photographs from NASA rovers to a minimal palette and naming them using online colour dictionaries.

Resources

http://chir.ag/projects/name-that-color/

https://codepen.io/meodai/full/mEvZRx

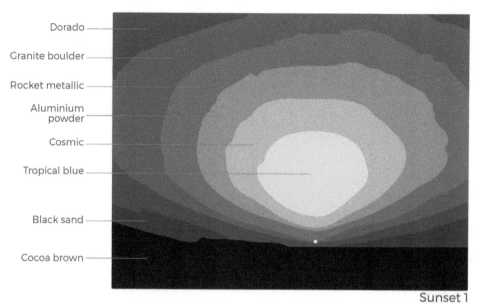

Dorado
Granite boulder
Rocket metallic
Aluminium powder
Cosmic
Tropical blue
Black sand
Cocoa brown

Sunset 1

Brass trumpet
Copper
Cathay spice
Milk chocolate

Rover tracks

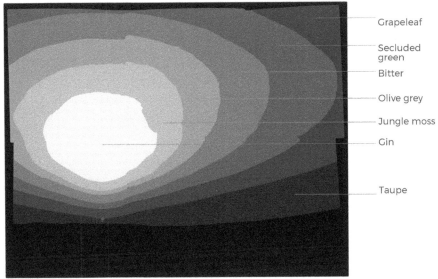

Grapeleaf

Secluded green

Bitter

Olive grey

Jungle moss

Gin

Taupe

Sunset 2

Roman coffee

Irish coffee

Old copper

Sepia skin

Peek-a-boo

Dr Elsa Bouet is currently a lecturer in English at Edinburgh Napier University. Her research focuses on dystopian fiction, science fiction, the Gothic and the New Weird. She is also a member of a Scottish research and creative network called Social Dimensions of Outer Space.

Red Journeys:
'Welcome to Planet Alba™!'
and the
Martian Literary Imaginary

Elsa Bouet

1. Red Conflicts: History and Bloodshed in 'Welcome to Planet Alba™!'

Pippa Goldschmidt's 'Welcome to Planet Alba™!' ('WPA') recasts the ways in which Mars is constructed and represented as the 'red planet' to portray global tensions that we risk reproducing there. In the story, a tourist attraction is designed to finance a spaceport built in a remote area of Scotland. The attraction offers a virtual-reality experience of what it feels like to be on Mars, where visitors can be 'alone on a planet and everything was shades of red'. As Ali, a newcomer working at the tourist attraction, explains, images of Mars obtained by three different rovers are compiled to create the virtual environment that tourists visit. Ali is surprised at the hues of the rovers' most up-to-date images of Mars as they are *not as red* as he was expecting. He too, despite being aware that recent photographs from the surface of Mars have captured a more orange and brown landscape, cannot shake off the idea that the planet is red.

However, he is not the only person guilty of still envisioning Mars as the red planet, a myth which the Visitor Centre is glad to keep selling to the tourists visiting the attraction, notably since management edits the images so that they look even redder after receiving a complaint from a visitor saying the images looked 'washed out'. This turns the virtual Mars into a 'cartoon-like' environment of bright blue skies and bright red rocks. 'WPA' redresses the misconception of the landscape as red and crowned with an earthly blue sky, which Sean McMahon also discusses in his piece, 'The R— Planet: What Colour is Mars?' The planet's true colour is more neutral, ranging from flesh to brown and gold. However, while 'WPA' deals with the misconstruction of the planet as red, it also employs myths associated with the colour red to explore some of the social, political and environmental issues that red Mars evokes, and which are commonly found in science fiction. In 'WPA', the planet's colour association does not lose its symbolic force, notably since both evoke the god of war: as Ali enters the simulation, he notices the redness of the planet, 'tinged red, the colour of clothing when it's been bloodied in a fight and not washed properly', hinting at conflict to come on Mars should we settle there, but also reflecting humanity's history of war.

The special suits that visitors wear provide a solitary experience of Mars, and while there might be family members and other visitors within the suite, each individual gets to experience Mars on their own. As people explore the virtual surface of Mars, they seem to be finding peace: ' And you could watch as everything fell away from them. All the annoyances about the long drive north to this place, and the bickering between the parents, and the kids mucking around in the back seat of the car and the staggering expense of the tickets to this place, they all disappeared'. Ali reflects that, 'I knew that if they were really there (on the real Mars and not on Mars Tomorrow™), they'd be arguing with each other about which crater to explore and how to set up camp and whose flag to fly and so on. And pretty soon it would just turn into the equivalent of one long tedious car journey': the experience of this new, pristine environment would not be enough to mesmerise and fulfil human curiosity, but instead, would cause fighting over colonisation rights as represented by the flags. No longer a place of utopian possibilities, the story is resigned to see Mars as a place where conflict, divisions and imperialism are to be exported.

2. Red Threats: Colonialism and Political Tensions

The association of the colour red with warfare is represented in H. G. Wells' *The War of the Worlds* (1898). At the opening of the novel, the narrator refers directly to the red colour of the planet, stating that 'Men like Schiaparelli watched the red planet – it is odd, by-the-bye, that for countless centuries Mars has been the star of war – but failed to interpret the fluctuating appearances of the markings they mapped so well' (ch.1). The novel here refers to Giovanni Schiaparelli, who mapped Martian channels in the 1870s. A couple of decades later, Percival Lowell thought these channels were the marks of an intelligent life capable of shaping its landscape.

The narrator of *The War of the Worlds* correlates the colour of the planet to the god of war and environmental destruction, as he states that the Martian planet is dying, since it is older and more remote to the sun than Earth. In a struggle to survive, the Martians have 'brightened their intellects, enlarged their powers, and hardened their hearts' (ch.1), and this pressing need to leave their planet in order to survive leads them to invade Earth. The narrator warns against judging Martians for their will to survive: 'And before we judge them too harshly we must remember what ruthless and utter destruction our own species has wrought, not only upon animals, such as the vanished bison and the dodo, but upon its inferior races' (ch.1). *The War of the Worlds* here uses the Martians to point to the destruction and warfare caused by humanity on Earth and condemns the expansionism which has led to the genocide of entire peoples. The novel then explicitly reveals its metaphor: 'Are we such apostles of mercy as to complain if the Martians warred in the same spirit?' (ch.1). Mars and Martians are here used as a mirror, one that decries bloodshed. As the novel ends, the narrator posits that 'we cannot regard this planet [Earth] as being fenced in and a secure abiding place for Man' (ch.10). While this suggests the threat of further invasion, the novel presents humankind as the biggest threat to itself because of the divisions it creates for itself. Indeed, in *A Modern Utopia* Wells sees a world at peace with itself since 'No less than a planet will serve the purpose of modern Utopia' (ch.13).

'WPA' recasts the political and social divisions that Wells critiques in his science fiction as it too represents global tensions.

Ali's thoughts often focus on fences: 'Me and fences didn't particularly get along'. Since he has emigrated to the US from a war-torn Arabic country, he understands isolation, displacement and the barriers that politics create. The spaceport is directly linked to the global context of divisions and war, since the Visitor Centre is described as 'defined' by its fence. Ali remembers 'the metal fences and tanks and military rockets lighting the night sky with fake stars' of his war-torn country, an image that correlates military rockets and space rockets, suggesting the risk of exporting our history of conflict into outer space.

The imagery of fences becomes more than an image of spatial separation and enclosure, and symbolises political divisions, notably since the Visitor Centre offers gimmicky passports to its visitors. This suggests that space is not imagined as a place of unity; rather, it is defined by 'international – *cosmic* – laws', by boundaries and hostilities we cannot transcend.

This global discord is portrayed through the tensions expressed towards the Chinese manned mission and presence in Scotland. This futurist story casts China as the next world power, having financially superseded the US and Britain, and symbolises a new form of imperialism, supplanting that of American or communist expansionism during the Cold War, which is represented in science fiction of the 1950s and 1960s, in which red Martians often stood for communists. China here serves a symbolic function, that of a country perceived as a threat, ironically reminiscent of how red Martians were linked to the Soviet Union in American science fiction of the Cold War. There is a trade agreement between China and Scotland, in that Chinese students are able to benefit from 'free tuition at Scottish universities, when, of course, the English and American ones were now off-limits to them (unless they could fork out the millions of yuan needed to get past the immigration paywall)', which is also the reason why the Scottish government succeeded in getting 'one of four non-Chinese licences to operate a tourist attraction' linked to the Chinese mission. Incidentally, the story associates crossing borders with wealth: wealthy Chinese students can study in America or England, just as wealthy tourists who can afford to travel to Scotland can afford the gimmicky passport to the VR suite and virtually access Mars; frontiers can be crossed by those who can afford it while others are left behind.

While there might be cooperation between countries, the reaching out to the Chinese astronauts by the tourists offers a form of hope in that it expresses a desire to connect with strangers, but ultimately connotes strife and the reproduction of conflict on Earth. As visitors are allowed to send messages and questions to the astronauts, we are told that McFadyan, one of the people working at the Visitor Centre, has to translate and filter out the disheartening, abusive, and possibly racist messages sent to them. The story gives the sense that while there is admiration for the Chinese astronauts, there is also resentment towards China: according to Susan, a lot of her lecturers at university were Chinese, and, to her, the real issue was not whether they could speak English but rather how 'fluent [students] were in Mandarin', a clear expression of antagonism towards the communist Chinese presence in Scotland, one that evokes a wider human propensity to fear or react against those they see as alien.

An origin of the association of Mars with communism can be found in Alexander Bogdanov's *Red Star: The First Bolshevik Utopia* (1908), which represents Mars as an advanced technological and communist society, having moved from a war-faring capitalist society. Written during the first Bolshevik revolution of 1905, Bogdanov's novel portrays a society in which communism has brought peace to the world and all individuals. It also represents the Martians as more advanced in comparison to Earth's divided society. The narrative retells the account of Leonid, an Earth scientist and revolutionist who is chosen to travel to Mars, to learn about its well-functioning society so that he can further the communist revolutionary efforts back in Russia and on Earth. As in Wells' narrative, Mars is a planet on the verge of death, as it is drying out, but the engineering efforts to build canals are seen as a way to save the planet. The Martians are also in search of a reliable energy source that will conserve their water and ensure their survival. While at a crucial stage of their survival, Bogdanov does not portray the Martians as conquering demons enacting the survival of the fittest through colonisation. Instead their superiority and capacity for peace is naturalised through the red Martian vegetation, which Leonid calls 'socialist vegetation' (Part II, ch.1), and the implementation of socialism and mutual aid is what will enable them to survive. One of the engineers on Mars also comments that the red hue of the vegetation on Earth is only masked by the stronger green colour (ibid.), which also suggests, as Wells does in *A Modern Utopia*, that unity is possible and desirable on Earth.

Subsequent American novels have also retained this association between Mars and socialism and communism, and the planet has been used as a metaphor for the Red Scare. Films from the 1950s and 1960s reflect the anxiety that communism is a threat to the individualism fostered by American capitalism: *Invaders from Mars* (1953), for example, casts the Martians as giant brain-like creatures with arms protruding from their heads coming in to take control of the American population, who become de-individualised automatons. This representation of Martians refers back to Wells' portrayal of them as giant-headed and short-limbed creatures presented in *The War of the Worlds*. Other films that link the Red Scare with Mars and Martians include *Flight to Mars* (1951), *The Angry Red Planet* (1959) and a film often voted among the worst ever made, *Santa Claus Conquers the Martians* (1964), in which Santa Claus liberates the Martians from the hold of their (communist) ideologies.

These films cast Martians as the communist threat to American freedom, reinforcing the idea that the country, capitalism and individualism are endangered by a totalitarian communism represented as homogenising everyone, in a way also reminiscent of John Wyndham's *The Day of the Triffids* (1951) in which the

Soviet Union has engineered plants that decimate the population of Britain. These narratives demonise the 'red alien' and promote political divisions and war instead of seeking commonalities and peace between different political beliefs.

However, not all fiction of the 1950s and 1960s represent the Martians as antagonistic; some articulate how political ideologies themselves become divisive. Ray Bradbury's *The Martian Chronicles* (1950) uses Mars to reflect on America's own sheltering, imperialist ideological system. Retracing the fictional colonisation of Mars by humans and the fate of the Martians, *The Martian Chronicles* presents several stories by different colonists depicting the violence the colonists are inflicting on their own and their descent into madness, while also addressing the Earthlings' exploitation of the planet. While doing so, the novel also tackles the homogenisation of the American dream and examines the boredom and blandness associated with the 1950s American vision of domesticity, which films such as *Invaders from Mars* celebrated. As the human invaders approach, the Martians feel a sense of doom that their peace is coming to an end. We see the Martian people attend a music recital: 'In the amphitheatres of a hundred towns on the night side of Mars the brown Martian people with gold coin eyes were leisurely met to fix their attention upon stages where musicians made a serene music flow up like blossom scent on the still air' (ch. 'August 1999'). Martian music reflects the peace and serenity achieved by this society who used to know war. As the Earthmen are approaching, the songs they sing carry words foreign to them, lyrics which they have acquired telepathically. Feeling unsettled by the knowledge that something is about to happen, they try to reassure themselves by saying that 'Nothing can happen to us. What could?' (ibid.) Having achieved social and political unity, they try to comfort themselves that war cannot happen, but it eventually does.

As the human settlers land and observe the former cities of the presumed-dead Martians, they sense that 'There is no hatred here', that the peacefulness can still be felt as 'they were a graceful, beautiful and philosophical people' (ch. 'June 2001'), knowing that their intact cities testify to the fact that life passed without waging war against one another.

Yet, despite this sense that life on Mars could be different from the atomically devastated Earth, a reference to both the bombing of Japan and the nuclear arms race of the Cold War, settlers suggest that Martian sites are likely to be renamed 'the Rockefeller Canal', that Earthmen 'have a talent for ruining big, beautiful things', that humanity is 'shouting with [its] play rockets and atoms', that 'Earth will be as Mars is today' (ibid.), deserted and dead, that mankind will bring about its own destruction on Earth and, in time, on Mars. The narrative further suggests atomic annihilation when it is said that the American government is planning to construct three atom bomb research facilities on Mars, ready to repeat the mistakes made on Earth, which have stemmed from creating ideological enemies.

3. Red Deserts: Environmental Issues

Bradbury's *The Martian Chronicles* attributes environmental destruction to political divisions and atomic warfare, and 'WPA' similarly connects environmental destruction and warfare. 'WPA' evokes our global history of war, notably through Ali's exile from the Middle East and his leaving the US, but it also invokes the Highland Clearances, the dislodging of Highland crofters to make way for sheep farming during the eighteenth and nineteenth centuries, which poses the question of who will be displaced as Scotland builds new spaceports.

During one of his walks, Ali stumbles upon a mossy pack of stones and then decides to take Susan, the co-worker he is attracted to, to visit the site. She is, though, reluctant to stay very long near the ruins as she states the place had been 'cleared', which explains why the land is so deserted and evokes Scotland's brutal history. However, Ali had himself wondered whether the Highlands had always been populated by sheep, 'minding their own business before the rockets arrived and barbequed them all', which have now been displaced and scorched by the spaceport to make way for technological progress. The narrative here indicates that the building of spaceports needs to be done with consideration as to who might be displaced in the process, and to consider the impact, both social and environmental, of space exploration, either here on Earth or on the planets we reach.

'WPA' also warns of further conflict to come, as water is becoming an increasingly scarce resource. Ali is struck by the amount of water in Scotland, since he had 'never lived in a place with so much obviously available water and so few people'. While this clearly refers to his native more arid Middle Eastern country, the story also suggests that there was not much water where he lived in the US. He ponders why people do not choose to emigrate to Scotland since 'people were fighting each other over water in other parts of the world'. This evokes images of a post-apocalyptic, drought-plagued Earth, captured in the *Mad Max* franchise (1979-2015), but also Isaac Asimov's 'The Martian Way' (1955) or Larry Niven's *Rainbow Mars* (1999). 'WPA' therefore hints at the possibility of further war due to water shortage, because of our lack of care for the environment, the destruction of which is portrayed to emanate from war as in Philip K. Dick's 'Survey Team' (1954).

'Survey Team' evokes the images of an arid Mars, like that seen in Wells and Bogdanov, but also portrays Earth as a wasteland. In this story, an eleventh-hour team from a devastated, war-torn Earth flies to Mars to see if it can provide a habitable environment for mankind and to survey the planet's resources. As they approach landing, they are able to see the planet and are surprised at the sight of canals, deserted cities and mining pits. However, the first questions the team asks themselves are 'Did they leave us anything?', 'Is there anything left for *us*?' and 'Is it all gone?', incredulous at the idea that Martians have used all their resources and that the team will have nothing to mine. These questions primarily suggest the team's sense of entitlement at exploiting the resources of the planet they seek to colonise. As the survey team explores the planet, the linguistics group discovers that the Martians did not die out but moved to another planet, and that their exodus did not go according to plan as 'they did not anticipate all the problems arising from colonization on a strange planet', notably a social breakdown that led to 'war, barbarism'. The team discovers that the Martians fled to Earth six thousand years prior to the survey team going to Mars; Earthlings are therefore the descendants of Martians returning to Mars. Having exploited the resources on Mars, the Martians fled to Earth which, they have plundered, leading to further wars.

The theme of dwindling water and food on Earth as a motive to colonise space is prevalent in science fiction, as in Asimov's *Robot Series* (novels which span from 1950 to 1985) in which Spacers are the descendants of the settlers who have left an overpopulated Earth. Kim Stanley Robinson also portrays these issues in his *Mars Trilogy* (1992–1996). In *Red Mars*, the first settlers on Mars, a team composed of carefully chosen scientists from the international community travelling on the *Ares*, reflect on the prospect of not repeating the history of Earth, remembering the 'waste, radiation, other people' (Part II), which echoes Asimov's representation of overcrowding on Earth, the threat of nuclear holocaust and the unsustainability of resource management. As this is being explained, one of the characters suggests that as scientists it is 'their job to think things new, to make them new', to have the desire and ethics to work towards a better system so as not to 'repeat all of Earth's mistakes just because of conventional thinking' (ibid.). Ironically, the team soon argues over the ways in which they could divide the tasks necessary to colonise and terraform Mars. Frank, the head of the American scientific team, states that he does not want to have arguments over the task allocation, as that is the type of argument he is trying to get away from, that is, he is trying to flee what ultimately symbolises political arguments with the Russian and Japanese teams. The novel directly links these global political conflicts to the god of war, as it was 'as if the god of war were really up there on that blood dot' (Part II), reminiscent of the 'bloodied' clothing of the virtual Mars in 'WPA'. These arguments take place on the *Ares* even before their mission to safeguard humanity really starts. As the crew disagrees on how to proceed with the exploration and terraforming of the planet, we learn that whatever the teams build on Mars will belong to the country who built it, while a UN treaty will allow any countries to visit any foreign facility, a system which could easily cause discord on Earth or Mars. As the crew discusses this set-up, they realise that they are still kept in 'the nightmare of Terran law' (Part II), the 'cosmic law' that 'WPA' refers to. The continuation of arguments among the scientific team pushes them to consider how they should go about colonising Mars or even if they should.

In *Red Mars*, Ann, an American geologist, suggests that the presence of humans will irretrievably change the face and the environment of Mars. As she and Nadia, a Russian engineer, explore the polar ice cap, she suggests that the planet was untouched since time began and that their presence on the planet has already changed it. However, they know that their work is to make '[r]roads, cities. New sky, new soil... and Mars will be gone and we'll be here, and we'll wonder why we feel so empty. Why when we look at the land we can never see anything but our own faces' (Part III). Ann suggests that the real Mars is almost unknowable because as soon as it is explored, it loses its authenticity to the human traces that are left in the process of exploration. To her, colonising the planet is not a process of inhabiting and adapting oneself to a new place, but rather of transforming the planet to humanity's needs, trying to recreate Mars in the image of a modernised Earth. Ann believes Mars will eventually be destroyed and humanity will have to live with itself knowing it destroyed and lost an entire ecosystem by changing it. As the terraforming of Mars becomes successful, and the Red planet is turned to blue and green (as indicated by the titles of the subsequent two novels, *Blue Mars* and *Green Mars*), Ann's initial doubt is confirmed and she becomes an environmentalist, being qualified as 'Red', symbolising both the mythical, arid colour of the planet but also her revolutionary politics, here opposed to the colour Green, a colour associated with progress, exploitation and environmental destruction on Mars. This ironically points to the need to be greener on the blue and green Earth. Ann's words are reminiscent of the warning formulated in 'Survey Team', in which both Mars and Earth have been ruined, and recall the cry of one of the team members not to further venture into space: 'Let's not destroy a third world!'

4. Conclusion

WPA' aptly reproduces the myth that Mars is the red planet, despite the recent rover discoveries that Mars is of paler colours, which the story acknowledges. Doing so serves an important symbolic function which mythically points to the god of war and in doing so evokes previous representations of the planet as an arid land, a warning against what could happen to our own planet, and also updates the metaphor to our current context.

Evoking the Mars of *The War of the Worlds*, but also of Cold War science fiction, in which the Martian aliens served to represent a colonial or ideological enemy, 'WPA' links the red planet to wider political arguments and war, both current and past. The constructed redness of the planet at the visitor centre highlights the human tendency to build fences, both geographical and political. The metaphor of the fences, linked to the red planet, allows the story to summon and criticise the history of human divisions, of exclusion and displacement, which we see in Ali's exile, the evocation of Middle Eastern conflicts, the Clearances, the resentment towards the Chinese presence in Scotland, which all serve to point to human propensity towards imperialism and conflict. The story connects this history of warfare to that of environment destruction. Deploying the image of Mars as red, it evokes the literary tradition of Mars as a dead planet, arid because of natural causes as in Wells or Bogdanov, or because of over-exploitation as in Dick and Bradbury. 'WPA' builds on this tradition by portraying an Earth that is experiencing water shortages, running the risk of becoming the red planet. As Alastair

Bruce notes in 'Mars: There and Back Again', it will be some time before we even send the first manned mission to Mars because of the difficulties of reaching the planet. And while that may be the case, 'WPA' questions whether we will be able to colonise it without causing conflicts among ourselves and without exploiting and destroying the planet. The story implicitly questions whether we should colonise Mars at all, as it also points to the systemic structural, ideological and environmental issues on Earth, which are represented as pressing, and thus suggests that we need to solve inequalities and divisions and care for one another and the planet, lest we destroy not another world but our own and ourselves.

List of work cited and suggested further reading:

Asimov, Isaac. *The Martian Way* (1955). London: Panther Books, 1974.

Bradbury, Ray. *The Martian Chronicles* (1950). London: Flamingo Modern Classics: 2008.

Bogdanov, Alexander. *Red Star: The First Bolshevik Utopia* (1908). Indiana: Indiana University Press, 1984.

Crossley, Robert. *Imagining Mars: A literary History*. Middletown: Weysleyan University Press, 2011.

Dick, Philip K. 'Survey Team' (1954) in *Second Variety: Volume Two of the Collected Stories*. London, Gollancz, 2003.

Flight to Mars. Selander, Lesley. Monogram Distr., 1951.

Invaders from Mars. Menzies, William Cameron, dir. Twentieth-Century Fox, 1953.

Markeley, Robert. *Dying Planet: Mars in Science and the Imagination*. Durham, NC: Duke University Press, 2005.

Niven, Larry. *Rainbow Mars*. New York: Tor, 2000.

Robinson, Kim Stanley. *Red Mars* (1992). London: Harper Books, 2009.

Santa Claus Conquers the Martians. Webster, Nicholas, dir. Embassy Picture, 1964.

The Angry Red Planet. Melchior, Ib, Dir. Sino Productions, 1959.

Wells, H.G. *The War of the Worlds* (1898). London: Penguin, 2018.

Wells, H.G. *A Modern Utopia* (1905). London: Penguin, 2005.

Wyndham, John. *The Day of the Triffids* (1951). London: Penguin, 2008.

Fringe in Space

Originally from California, **Laura Lam** now lives in Scotland. She is the author of the Micah Grey trilogy (starting with *Pantomime*), the Pacifica cyberpunk thrillers (starting with *False Hearts*), and short pieces such as work in *Nasty Women* and *Cranky Ladies of History*.
Her next books are *Goldilocks*, about the first all-female space mission to an exosolar planet to save humanity from a dying Earth, and a co-written far future space adventure, *Seven Devils*, which has been described as *Mad Max: Fury Road* in space.
Laura lectures part-time on the Creative Writing MA at Edinburgh Napier University.

A Certain Reverence

Laura Lam

Day 1

We left Earth today.

My ma drove me up to Sutherland Spaceport herself, and I left Edinburgh behind. The smog was bad for my last day on the planet, tinging everything a sickly yellow. Not many cars on the road, just those creaky cargo trekkers. Ma held my hand the whole way, as if I was still a wee girl. The government ordered us a much nicer car than we could have borrowed. No glitches in the self-guide. No getting lost. No sputtering off to the side of the road half the time because the old censors didn't know it needed a charge.

When we arrived, my ma gave me the strongest hug and a face full of her curly black hair. Her dark brown hands gripped my lighter brown ones, leaving paler indents on my skin.

She gave me a little present, wrapped in plastic, and told me to open it once we lifted off. Once Earth was just a little speck in the sky. Open it and think of me, she said, and I'll be thinking of you.

She got me then. I had to give her one last squeeze then hoof it, or else I'd start bawling right in front of my new crew.

My ma almost stopped me going. They'd already made an exception for my age (next youngest on board is twenty-five compared to my nineteen), but she could have overruled it. She let me go in the end, though. Even if it means I'll never see her again. Even if I went there and immediately back again, 44 years will pass on Earth. She'd be pushing 100. She could be a stubborn enough old biddy to make it that long. Or the aliens will give us the secret to eternal life, and I'll never have to lose her at all.

My ma gave the chef all her recipes, made her promise to make them for me on my birthday. From stovies to groundnut stew. From cranachan to puff puff. Didn't have the heart to tell her we'd mostly be eating astronaut food. Lots of things out of packets.

Leaving Earth was like all the practice runs and yet nothing like 'em. We all screamed as we left the atmosphere. Fifty-two souls on board. The sound almost drowned out the roar of the engines.

Earth must be a little speck now, though there are no windows, not with the speed we're going. I unwrapped the present. It's so cheesy. A cross-stich, the cloth dyed like a galaxy of purple, blue, and pink. A few white stars, and then, across the middle:

HOME SWEET HOME

Had to laugh. It's perfect though. Already hung it up above my bunk. That speck of Earth is everything I ever knew, already thousands of miles away.

It was only after the first ship arrived after a forty-year journey that the Proxis gave us speed-of-light tech so we could send the next round of ships and missions. The first ship was Chinese, American, and Russian crew. Must have been something, to land on what you think is an empty planet only to find out the aliens were there all along. Surprise! Time for first contact.

The real kicker is the Proxis had already come and observed us over the centuries, none of us any the wiser. They watched as we suffocated the world. Let us carry on with it. Arseholes.

I mean, being the first humans to 'discover' aliens is cool and all, but it also must have felt pretty shite for those who did the Starshot mission. Spend forty years of your life in space only to realise you could have made it in a tenth of the time if these aliens had felt like sharing. Then again, the astronauts/cosmonauts could go home when they thought they'd die in space or on an empty planet. So that's something.

The Proxis want to learn more of us, see our ways, our culture. We're the Scotland ship. Most countries have launched their own, though a few are sharing to save resources. Scotland's always dead set on doing it our own way, though, aren't we?

So we're all headed to this planet circling that dull red star to show them all this corner of humanity has to offer. And in return, we find out if they're going to help us. And even if they help us, who's to say we'll get back in time to find there's any Earth left to save?

-Blair

31 October 2035

Official log of crewmember Blair Orji, acrobat, singer, and research assistant.

Day 29: We're all settled into Kinnara-3, our new space home. I helped double-check inventory with Junior Scientist Kenneth Callahan. We tested the suits, ensured all our radiation goggles are in working order, and every member on crew is continuing their research. I'm starting with general knowledge then I'll figure out what I'll specialise in.

Science fiction films have it all wrong, I'm sad to report. One, we're not allowed to actually look at the stars because we'd be fried from radiation. But even if we could see them, the stars wouldn't look like threads or a tunnel when you move close to the speed of light. All we'd see is a hazy grey orb—residual radiation from the Big Bang. We'd see the cosmic microwave background blueshifted into the visible and the stars would be blueshifted to X-Ray. These are the types of things I'm learning on this ship.

The stars are invisible, but they're still there.

Back on Earth, where you are, time's passing differently. We're going 98% the speed of light, so our journey will feel like slightly longer than 4.24 light years—it'll technically be 4.33 years. But for you back on Earth, 22 years will pass. I'm not sure I'll ever get my head around it.

We've already received contact from the a Proxi alien. It's basically an email, but thanks to their tech it arrives instantly rather than after years. They won't share the mechanisms, but I can send and receive messages back home thanks to the same tech, and I'm grateful for that.

He'll (I mean, he's been using male pronouns, but that doesn't exactly translate into Proxi gender and sexuality) be interacting with all of us as we make our way towards him and his planet.

There are small charged particles hurtling through space at the speed of light. The Proxis gave us shielding because a shipful of dead humans arrive is likely less interesting to them. I'm conducting experiments with the other scientists on the ship to try and discover how it works. I've attached a sample equation. This is an example of the type of things we work on up here in space.

Until next time!

Click here to see Blair's calculation!

Day 334

Haven't updated this since the first night almost a year ago. We have to make so many official logs back to Earth that the last thing I want to do is sit and actually write longhand. I hate those logs now. Have to write 'em knowing they're going to be read by millions of humans is hard. We're supposed to sound all formal yet conversational at the same time.

Some of my crewmen are really, really honest with what life is like on the ship. But most of us self-censor and are pretty damn boring. Today I studied this. Today I calculated that. Today I ran this experiment. I like the work, but writing up the results for those back home feels fake. I have to tone down the Scottishness because Americans don't follow it.

Turns out I'm ready to scribble away in this thing when I'm in a flap. So here we go.

Kenny the Bastard Junior Scientist told the heid Science Officer herself I was 'difficult to work with', just because I corrected him on a calculation about the shields. What he neglected to tell the Science Officer – and I kept my own mouth shut about since I'm no a grass – was he said he wouldn't be corrected by no huddy.

Aye, I'd heard what some of them called us. Huddies. The ones who knew a wee bit of science but were learning more on the way. They chose some of us because of what we could offer on the performance side. The dancers, the singers, the acrobats, like me. I'm only on this ship because I'm bendy and can do three flips in a row. That's only what a couple of them think, anyway. And plenty of the boffins are learning acting or singing or studying up on their Rabbie Burns.

So aye, I bit back at him. He's just mad that the alien Proxi contact for our ship, Gall, writes to me more than him. Not my fault Kenny is boring. And he won't get chosen to perform in front of the Proxis. He'll only see them from afar, if at all.

Poor, wee Kenny. Tch.

-Blair

Day 989

Transcript of conversation with crewmember Blair Orji and Proxi Contact D-3, alias Gall.

Blair: Why do you talk to me more than the other members of the crew?

Gall: You ask the most questions.

Blair: Ah, so you like the bolshy ones. OK. Here's a question: are you looking forward to meeting us? Or are you like ugh, humans, crashing our planet, pure annoying.

Gall: 'Looking forward to.' That is such a human way of phrasing it.

Blair: What's the alien way?

Gall: I believe it would translate to the idea that we view your coming as a gift that we will receive with reverence.

Blair: Right.

Gall: You're holding something back.

Blair: I'm wanting to say something cheeky, but it doesn't matter. I did another calculation. I know this is like a kid showing you their crayon drawing—I mean, even to the other humans—but will you receive my gift with reverence?

Gall: Humans don't have a monopoly on sarcasm. But yes, I will gladly.

Blair: Nice one.

Day 1366

Had one of those shite practice sessions today where nothing clicked. Did my warm-up. Plenty of stretching. Worked with coach (and lead of Astrophysics) on flip technique. He made me do a handstand for two minutes! Thought I was going to fall on my heid by the end. Coach says I keep tilting my heid to the side when the movements get tough. Must work on that. Though would the aliens really gie a toss?

Did eighty minutes on silks. Then cool down. Finally. Whole body feels like jelly. Been awhile since coach put me through my paces like that. We've been up in the stars for almost eight months now. They say artificial gravity is the same, but it's not. I move differently up here.

Just had a tidy scran of shite outta a packet and now it's rec. Going to nap. Then it's singing practice. Today's creative. Back to the science tomorrow. Sent Gall a message, but he hasn't responded. Maybe because we're getting closer. Or maybe he finds me dull as a doornail.

I want to call my mam. She's good at talking me down when I get in a faff. She does wish she'd kept me back, though she never says it. It floats there between us though. She's turning 63 back on Earth any time now. Better call her before I nap—could sleep through it.

-Blair

Day 1580

We're landing tomorrow. Tonight, we're circling Proxima Centauri b, which the Proxis themselves call something we cannae even hope to pronounce. Spent the last few years trying to get some sort of handle on Proxi linguistics, but our throats are never going to master it. Turns out aliens like bagpipes because they sound the closest to their language, ain't that a laugh?

At least from all my hard work I can understand a few of the Proxi language recordings now. It does sound a bit like someone put a tennis ball in a blender.

I wanted to learn enough to say 'Hi, how are you?' to Gall. Don't think I'll manage.

It'll be weird to meet him, the one who interrogated us under the guise of being our new alien chum. Never knew what answers he wanted me to give. He liked my shite banter, so I gave him plenty of it.

Proxima Centauri b does look pretty from up here. It's tidal locked, so half of it is always darker than the devil's waistcoat, as my gran liked to say, and the other half is burned to a crisp. We're landing in the Twilight Zone since that's the only place humans can survive. Even the Proxis don't go on the surface of nightside or dayside—they stay in the subterranean lattice underneath the entire planet to protect themselves from the solar storms. When we lower into the atmosphere, it's definitely alien. We're able to lift the shields on the windows for the first time in over four years.

The Proxima Centauri sun is dim. From the planet it looks larger than ours, all red and hazy, but the actual sun is a wee thing, with a radius a tenth of the size of our sun. The binary star of Alpha Centauri blaze in two, tiny pinpoints, right next to each other from where we're looking. The oceans and mountains are jagged, broken teeth. Look at me, trying to be all figurative in my writing. My ma would be proud.

Haven't been able to talk to Ma much recently. Even though the Proxis shared the tech, it still takes so long for the Scottish Space Agency to comb through it before sending it to her, then they look at it all again before they send back. Nosy buggers.

The videos always come eventually, even if sometimes they're scrambled and Ma sounds like a robot. In each one, she's that much greyer, that much more lined. But I look the same.

It'll be cold planetside. I'm so used to being on a starship programmed to be perfect for humans. Down there, even in the twilight zone, it'll be 8°C. No frozen water, but even on an alien planet it's going to be dreich weather. Hah.

The gravity is higher than Earth. Our suits will help keep us warm, protect us from the radiation, do what they can for the gravity when we're not in the human quarters on Proxima. The aliens can shift gravity whenever they want underground, evidently. Means if we get on their tits, it'd be easy enough to nix us.

This all feels like a joke. We package up what makes humans great and the aliens make their call. Are we even selling 'em the real thing? Or is it like the fake tat we tout at the tourists, which isnae anything like true Scotland at all?

It doesn't feel like home. Part of me doesn't want to go down. I havenae told anyone, and it's hard to even write it in here, but I'm afraid of the aliens. Of what they'll be like. Why would they even want to save us?

Even though we've spoken most days for two years, and even though I've learned more from him than my own mentors, I'm a little afraid of Gall.

-Blair

Day 1581

This has been a day.

I knew meeting an alien would be weird. But it was still way weirder than I expected.

Only the humans who live permanently on Proxima ever see the aliens as they are. Despite all the folk back home bitherin them to snap a photo, no one's cracked. Tabloids back home keep publishing fakes.

I knew the Proxis would use their humanoid avatars. None of us have a clue what they're made of—clones or androids or mouldable goo, fuck knows. They say they do it to make us more at ease. Just means we imagine them all the more monstrous.

Took ages to put on the suit and actually get off the spaceship where we've spent the last four years. That first step on alien soil, though. That was something.

We all said 'one giant step for mankind' as we touched down. Think we all grew a little space crazy, near the end. Knowing this was coming. We're still breathing artificial air, we can't feel the atmosphere on our skin. I wonder what the planet smells like.

We only spent an hour on the surface. The sky was all blue and pink. The planet's tidally locked—no sunrise or sunsets in the Twilight Zone. The rocks were striated, pointed at the top, like the Quiraing but in colours of dull fire instead of green, black, and the purple of heather. No plant life, no other animals. Dinnae know how anything could survive here at all.

Below ground is a different story. It was warmer down there, though still baltic for humans. The suit kept me toasty enough, but ice frosted the edges of the caves and tunnels, the striped rock carved smooth. Our muffled steps echoed as we twisted our way to the meeting place. Light came from red, glowing fungus-like plants. Aye, it looked real evil.

So I was pure gobsmacked to see a man dressed up in full Scottish Jacobite garb in the middle of the underground alien tunnel. No word of a lie. Kilt, sporran, red socks, white ruffled shirt, a cap with a bloody fake thistle in it—the works! Like he was about to run across the field at Culloden.

All fifty of us stopped and stared. Kenny fainted, and I almost guffawed at that. They had to send him back to the ship.

I don't think anyone could really process what was happening. Whatever we were expecting when we came face to face with an alien, it wasnae this. I couldn't help it—I laughed. His heid swivelled towards me. Eyes were too green.

Gall.

He gave us a hearty hello, and he had something resembling a Scottish accent, but it was all tilted. Hard to put your finger on why, but once we were close enough to him, he could only just pass for human. His skin was just that bit too smooth. Those green eyes didn't blink often enough. Ginger whiskers too even. Uncanny valley.

Gall kept turning his heid towards me. I was all self-conscious; my face was a sweaty mess within my helmet. One of my braids was in my face that I couldnae move aside. Gall gave something meant to be a smile.

The Captain spoke to our Jacobite, polite like, though I bet his heart was hammering as fast as mine. There was much pomp and circumstance. I wanted to talk to him. Have a conversation that wasn't recorded to be dissected and disseminated. Ask him what I really wanted to know: where were the aliens? Were they all watching us, somehow? What does he really want from us? From me?

The back of my neck prickled.

Gall took us through more winding corridors until we entered a large arena. This is where we'd perform. They'd carved it special. The stands were all in shadow. They would seal this area off, pump it full of oxygen so we could perform without the suits. Amend the gravity, like they do in the human quarters.

The Captain wasnae good at hiding his greed and hope. That the aliens will gie us what we need. Knowledge. Tech. Power. The key to changing our dying world. Plugging up our punctured atmosphere. Our bairns growing up. If they don't help, then in no time we're all refugees, hoping these aliens let us claim sanctuary anyway.

We all had to go to the ship psychologist after meeting the aliens. I found it a waste of time. Yeah, aliens are weird. Who knew? Think others took it harder, though. Guess I ken that.

Have to go practise. Feels like all I do is push my body to its limits and then push my brain just as hard. Cannae remember the last time I just . . . was.

-Blair

Day 1583

Finally had a chance to talk to Gall face to face. Still I dunno how to feel about being one of his 'chosen' crewmen. Half-honoured, half-suspicious. He took his time, picking through the crew. One day, he talked to the Captain. The next to a scientist, then a singer. Finally, the acrobat.

The crew slept on the ship. We'd gone down to the human settlement, clustered in the Twilight Zone. Full of the people from the first mission who had decided not to go back to Earth. Their bairns, who'd never known Earth at all.

Life on Proxi still took its toll, despite alien tech. They wore goggles to see better in the dimness. They even ate the glowing fungus the aliens did. I tried some—it tasted beyond foul. Like rubbish even the Edinburgh seagulls wouldn't touch.

Some of the humans spoke some weird blend of a humanoid Proxi. I could follow along, had some conversations with them. These folk are changed, though. I wasnae sure if they felt like kin. But they seemed happy enough, on this cold rock so far from home. They had the option to come back to Earth, if they wanted, but so far none had volunteered.

My first few chats with Gall, when he finally called for me, were just like when we sent messages on the ship. I watched what I said, and he was dead evasive.

Gall likes to play at being human. He's really hamming it up. I wonder how much of himself he tucks away. Reading between the lines, his species have extra senses he cannae even describe to us because they're so far beyond our ken. They see more on the infrared spectrum than us. He tried to project an image to me of how he viewed me. Kinda looked like I was made of fire, which was, to be honest, pretty ace.

Finally asked him why he appeared so overbearingly Scottish to meet us. Didn't he realise that while we all love our country, Too Scottish things are always aimed at the tourists, not us?

He cocked his heid, fake thistle bobbing, and my suit turned off. The lights went dark. I clawed at the handheld on my wrist, desperately trying to reboot, imagining suffocating and my heid exploding.

Relax, the alien told me. Said I could breathe in here just fine and might as well take off my helmet. They were upgrading the caverns, so they could make any area underground human-friendly, rather than only the area with the original settlers.

Every science fiction film I'd seen told me that was a bad idea, but I did as he asked. The air smelled braw. Crisp, cold, damp with the smell of fresh water and deep earth. I hadnae smelled real air in years, and never anything so clean.

Gall leaned against the smooth wall. The last time he'd been to Earth had been during the Jacobite era, and he still had a fondness for it. He'd spent twenty years in Scotland before he came back. I dinnae know how he would have passed as human. Maybe his avatar back then was missing a few more teeth and a bit ragged 'round the edges.

I asked how old he was and received an elegant shrug as an

answer. I guess that means ancient.

Couldnae help asking what he really looked like, half-afraid, half-curious. If he burst out of his fake human suit into some Cthulhu monster, I would officially lose my shite.

He smirked as if he guessed my thoughts. Said we wouldn't be able to see much of them, if he showed me. Outside our light spectrum.

I can't hope to describe it in your language, he said, and you can't learn ours enough to understand. So let me be as I am. Here. Now.

I could only blink at that.

He pointed out my suit wasn't recording anymore, so we could have a real conversation that no one could hear. Even writing down the gist of it here now I'm back in the ship feels like a risk. Dinnae want anyone to find this, but I dinnae want to forget.

So I asked him why all this pomp? Why make us put everything into sending ships across the stars to perform for them? If they've already been to Earth, they know what humans are like. That we're cruel and kind and stubborn and never sure of ourselves. They know our art, our cultures. What's different about making a ragtag group of performers-slash-scientists essentially put a Fringe show out on the fringes of the universe?

Much of it was above his head, Gall told me, but they had a plan.

Vague as fuck, right? I told him they're toying with us, that we're mice and they're the cats.

He asked me if I thought humanity deserves to be saved.

And that stopped me short. Because aye, of course, I think we do. But how to say why?

He kept blethering. I'll try to write it as close as I remember:

—Say we give you this technology you require. What do you do with it? Do you heal your planet only to start killing it again? Kill each other? Your planet is already overcrowded. You've made some progress in terraforming, but it'd take generations for Mars to be habitable. And what then—you keep spreading your violent, selfish ways through the universe? Is what we give you a weapon or a gift? If we save you, do you consider us your kings, your oppressors, your gods?

His questions rained down on me. I don't know the answers to any of 'em. I'm just one lass. I can't speak for humanity. A lot of what he said made a sick sort of sense. There've been times where I've wondered if we're worth it, but then there's some spark that shows just how amazing we humans can be.

He said he didn't expect me to have the answers. That, perhaps, there were no answers. But that he and the others were still looking forward to our show.

Then I realised that this wasnae the first time they had made this call.

His heid tilted up at that, bathed in the red glow.

–Do you really think we're the only two species out here?

–And what, you study all of them, deciding which ones are worth helping, if they need it, and which to turn away?

–Maybe you should stay, then. After your crewmen leave. You'd be able to understand us better.

–Stay on a planet with people who don't care if we die, I said. So tempting.

He smiled and passed me a little orb, stored in his sporran. It was pretty, made from the striped rock of the planet, polished to a high shine. Like a mini-model of Proxi.

I thanked him for it, but I also wanted to throw it at his heid.

–If we helped you and you knew your Earth was safe, would you stay?

I considered, my heart hammering.

I asked him what I could do here. My science wasn't great. I didn't really jive with the other humans who'd been here for generations. Three had decided to go back.

–You could do what you liked. Learn about other stars, other worlds.

–Other aliens? I asked.

–Maybe, he said with a sly smile.

I hmmed, not giving him an answer, but thanking him for the orb. I put my helmet on, desperate to return to my crew.

The last thing I said to him was that I couldn't speak for all of humanity, but I could speak for me. And I would consider the gift of life something worth all the reverence I could give.

He let me leave.

-Blair

Day 1589

We performed.

There's something that happens when the day you've been anticipating for years actually comes to pass. It never lives up to that shiny, sparkling dream in your mind. Nothing ever goes smoothly.

And we performed in a seemingly empty auditorium, except for the small cluster of the Proxi humans in a corner.

Evidently the aliens were all there, crushed to the gills (I don't know if they actually have gills – my guess is nah). The rafters were shadowed, and we might not have been able to view them anyway. We all imagined monsters.

Still put on the best show we could. We twisted, twirled. They'd installed silks and I climbed them, hung upside down, my legs in a split, blood rushing to my heid. The music played and swirled, acoustics amazing in that underground cavern. I wore my fitted, sparkling leotard, the star of Proxima Centauri stitched to my left shoulder, Proxima Centauri b marking a stitched orbit around my torso, the planet on my ribs. Me and the other acrobats and dancers moved through the choreography. On the trapeze, I caught Damien, and his hands were slippery despite the chalk. He didnae fall, and neither did I.

Mindy the contortionist twisted into impossible shapes. By the end of it, we'd performed basically a full circus, minus the animals and the clowns (because I'm nae convinced clowns are gonna persuade 'em humanity is worth saving). After we finished the acrobat section, I moved into singing, my voice rising through the auditorium.

I sang a mixture of traditional Scottish ballads. Trevor, our baritone, joined me in the duets. We sang popular songs (aye, we sang the Proclaimers even though we've gone a hell of a lot further than five hundred miles). When my bit was done, we put on our other shows. At the comedy, the humans laughed, but we had no idea if the aliens did. The scattered human applause felt so quiet in the grand, empty space.

Some of the others put on an adaptation of *Caledonia*, and another put on *Wicked*. I did see one of the humans wipe away a tear, and that was something.

I cannae even bring myself to write all we did. Just this much has worn me out. It went on for hours. We put everything we had into every performance. So much work, so much sweat and tears and heartache. We'd travelled across the galaxy but it seemed as empty as a shite Fringe show no one wanted to see.

As the never-ending twilight of the Proxi planet wore on, we wilted.

At the end, as we bowed and rose back up, still panting. The humans, bless 'em, gave it their all, and I beamed over at them.

We'd pleased our own kind, to be sure, but we still had no clue what the aliens thought.

Gall came forward. Tilted his heid again. And he clapped. Once, twice, three times, then faster. The humans joined in again, even louder than before. Some gave cheers.

Though we still saw none of the aliens in the rafters, the walls began to shake in a patter of noise.

The aliens applauded us. Better late than never.

Our tired soldiers straightened, we beamed at the darkness. We took another bow.

Gall grinned at us, showing his too-white, too-even teeth.

He told us he accepted our gift with open arms.

Then he sent us back to the ship to await our fate.

Tosser.

I left a message for my ma. She's already 67 now.

-Blair

Day 1590

This morning, we still didnae have our answer.

I'm still thinking about Gall's offer of staying.

I met with him again, another non-recorded blip. Last time, the crew was well freaked out my suit had malfunctioned. They'd given me a brand new one, yet with a blink of an eye, Gall turned it dark and I breathed the fresh air again.

The cavern pulsed red from the creepy fungus. Water dripped.

We were so far underground. Above us was the beginnings of the dayside part of the planet, scorched dry. Every eleven days, we orbited that red dwarf. Each night, the stars changed. I'd helped the astronomers map it. A couple of days of every eleven, we face towards Earth. You can see our star, but not our planet. I always blew my ma a kiss.

I'd brought Gall's gift with me, twisting the orb this way and that.

If I stayed and learned about the aliens, I asked him, would I be deciding their fate, too?

Gall shrugged, an oddly human gesture. He said it wasn't likely. Only happened once a millennia or so.

–Ah yes, I said, bitter. I'm only a blip to you. A tiny, interesting ant.

–No, Gall said. You're so much more.

Gall leaned forward, his hands on his knees. And I swear, for a moment, he glimmered. His skin flashed red, orange, yellow. Like the fired version of myself in infrared. A different shape unlike anything I could describe. Tendrils, looping over each other, spiralling out, like a mini-galaxy.

Gall showed me himself. Bright and glorious. Then he disappeared back into his simulacrum of a man.

He reached out a hand, closed my fingers around the orb.

–I gave you our answer before you ever performed, he said. We made up our mind before you even landed. We enjoyed the show, just the same.

Then he was gone.

-Blair

Day 1691

The spacecraft leaves in an hour.

Everyone's all loaded up, ready to speed back to Earth to save it. I don't know if the ship will arrive in time. But we can try.

I was all packed, all set, all ready to go. Twenty-two years outside the ship, four and a bit years inside, and I'd be back on that sickly planet. Maybe my ma would still be kicking, maybe she wouldn't. We'd only spent a few months here, rather than the year or two we'd mapped out, a lengthy courtship with the aliens until we wore them down and they gave us what we wanted.

When I walked up to the Captain and handed him the orb a week ago, he didn't know what to make of it. Almost scoffed until I held it in my hands and it started syncing with our computers. Hell if I know how it works, but it stores an infinite amount of scientific stuff. As the information streamed up on the screen, he sobbed. Everyone on board did. I stood there, thinking I'd howl but feeling ... I don't know. Like it wasnae enough.

The sour look on Bastard Kenny's face was worth it though. He'd been completely useless on this mission. Kenny can fuck off.

Everyone else was lovely. I got picked up, twirled around. Performer-scientists and scientist-performers alike. We had a massive party on board. Some of the Proxi-humans from the first ship came. Gall and a couple of other Proxi-avatars came too, amused by the sight of humans on the lash.

I'm sitting on the craft now, in my wee cabin. I've my ma's cross-stitch in my lap, left hand running along the even stitches.

I really didn't think I'd want to stay. There's a lot of minuses:

Cold

Aliens are weird, though not as bizarro as I first thought

Ditto to the other humans

Red mushrooms are disgusting

No ma?

No one else from our ship decided to stay. I'm not even sure if they asked. They wanted to go home, and I get that. I do. But Earth had nothing for me but my ma.

I phoned her up yesterday. Her hair's pure white now. She's still a stunner.

She always smiles so big when she sees me.

I showed her the cross stitch and she laughed. She said she barely remembered making it. I guess it was a long time ago, for her.

She noticed when my face went all solemn.

–What do you want to ask, child?

–Are you mad, that I dinnae want to come back to Earth?

She shook her head and told me of course not. She'd known since I was two I was a girl who liked to wander. But she missed me every day.

Time to ask. I took in a deep breath.

–My mate Gall, he said they could bring you here, if you wanted. I know it's a hell of a step, and you have so much back out there and I'm selfish to ask but—

She held up a hand and cut me off. Said she'd have her bags packed and they could come get her as soon as they liked. That she'd only been waiting and hoping for me to ask.

Gall sent a ship out right away. It'll still take almost nine years before she's hear. Turns out even the aliens cannae go faster than the speed of light. She'll be thirty years older than when I last saw her.

She's coming, though, and I cannae wait.

But until then, there's plenty to keep me busy.

There's a universe out here.

-Blair

Dr. Beth Biller is a Reader at the Institute for Astronomy of the University of Edinburgh. Beth specializes in the direct detection and characterization of exoplanets – taking pictures of planets that circle other stars and using the resulting data to determine their size, composition, and weather.

Life, but not as we know it: the prospects for life on habitable zone planets orbiting low-mass stars

Beth Biller

The habitable zone, and how to find planets in it

In the last 25 years, astronomers have detected thousands of planets orbiting stars other than our Sun, by both direct and indirect means. The diversity of these planets is staggering. For example, we have detected: "Hot Jupiters", planets more massive than Jupiter hugging their suns, with orbital periods of days instead of years; "Super-Earths and Mini-Neptunes", planets in between Earth and Neptune in size, a type of planet that does not exist in our own Solar System; and many more. We have detected planets in almost every separation and mass regime for which we have the sensitivity to detect planets.

Amongst this diversity in exoplanets, we have now detected a small cohort of planets residing in the habitable zone around their star. The habitable zone is the range of orbits around a given star where a planet, should it have sufficient atmospheric pressure, could potentially have liquid water on its surface [9]. Having an orbital separation which places it in the habitable zone is the minimum requirement for a planet to potentially host life. For stars with masses similar to the Sun, the habitable zone is located (unsurprisingly) right around 1 AU (astronomical units) – the average distance of the Earth from the Sun. For higher mass stars, which burn hotter and are larger than the Sun, the habitable zone will move outwards to larger orbital separations. For lower mass stars, which are conversely cooler and considerably smaller than the Sun, the habitable zone is located at comparatively smaller orbital separations. The two best-known habitable zone planetary systems to date are Proxima Centauri [1] and the planets orbiting the star

TRAPPIST-1 [6].

The closest stars to us after the Sun are the triple system of Alpha Centauri A and B and Proxima Centauri. Proxima Centauri is the closest of the three, at a distance of 4.2 light years from the Earth. Proxima Centauri is a red dwarf, with a mass of about a tenth of the Sun. While Alpha Centauri A and B are very bright stars in the Southern sky (and similar in mass to our Sun), Proxima Centauri is much fainter than its two companions and was only discovered in 1915. Anglada-Escud é et al. 2016 [1] discovered an exoplanet companion in orbit around Proxima Centauri b by measuring the slight wobble of the star due to the gravitational pull of the planet on the star. We commonly think of planets as orbiting stars, but the pull of gravity goes both ways, with the planet exerting an equal and opposite force on the star. For a star-planet system, where the star will be much more massive than the planet, the centre of mass will fall within the star, and the star will appear to "wobble" due to the influence of the planet. By measuring the frequency of this wobble, we can measure the orbital period of the planet. The degree to which the star wobbles then tells us something about the mass of the planet. For the planet Proxima Centauri b, we have measured an orbital period (a Proxima "year") of 11 days and a lower limit on mass of 1.3x the mass of the Earth. Since Proxima Centauri (the star) is quite low mass, this places the planet within the habitable zone of this star. But this is literally all we know about this planet – how long its year is, and a lower limit on its mass. Clearly, this is insufficient to determine if it is actually habitable.

The planets around TRAPPIST-1 [6] were detected differently, via the transit technique. This technique requires a very particular geometry – if the planet passes directly between us and the star along our line of sight, it will block some (very small) amount of starlight. This is known as a transit event. Since we have a relatively good idea of the size of the star from computer modelling of stars, the fraction of starlight blocked is then related to the size of the planet. Transit events will repeat once an orbit – thus the frequency of observed transits will yield the orbital period ("year") of the planet. The deepest transits observed to date are for "Hot Jupiter" planets, which block at most 1% of the light of the star, but most observed transits are much shallower than this. Clearly, choosing small stars to observe will make it easier to detect a transit, as a planet will block proportionally more light when transiting across a smaller versus a larger star. TRAPPIST-1 is one such extremely small star which is ideal for transit studies – so ideal that Gillon et al. 2017 [6] detected a full system of 7 different planets orbiting this star! Three of the TRAPPIST-1 planets (TRAPPIST-1c, d, and e) have orbits which place them in the habitable zone. In particular, TRAPPIST-1e appears to have a size, mass, and density similar to the Earth [7], but we still have insufficient information to determine if any of these planets are truly habitable. However, the TRAPPIST-1 planets in particular are excellent candidates for follow-up spectroscopy with the soon-to-be-launched James Webb Space Telescope.

Proxima Centauri b and TRAPPIST-1bcdefg are the most famous of the current cohort of habitable zone exoplanets – altogether, there are roughly 20 planets currently known that reside in the habitable zone around their star. The vast majority of these orbit stars are less massive than the Sun. This is mostly due to the fact that these planets are considerably easier to detect than habitable zone planets around higher mass stars (as discussed above), but such planets appear to be quite common. Thus, it is worth evaluating whether they are truly habitable or just in the potentially habitable zone.

2. What would a habitable zone planet orbiting a low mass star be like?

From what we know about low mass stars and the orbits of these planets, we can speculate regarding conditions on habitable zone planets around low mass stars, and how they may differ from our own planet. One key difference might be how one would tell time on such a planet. We delineate time via both the rotational period ("day") and orbital period ("year") of our planet. In contrast, Proxima Centauri b has a "year" of 11 days, and the TRAPPIST-1 planets have "years" of 1–20 days! These planets are also so close to their stars that they are most likely tidally locked. This means that one side of the planet always faces the star, while the other always faces away. In this case, the rotational period of the planet is the same as the orbital period – in other words, the length of a "day" is the same as the length of a "year". (A nearer example of tidal locking is the orbit of the Moon – the same side of the Moon always faces the Earth. The first image of the far side of the Moon was only taken in 1959, by the Soviet Union's Luna 3 spacecraft.)

A result of tidal locking is that the "time of day" observed then becomes dependent on what part of the planet you are on, as there will be a dayside and a nightside, separated by a thin strip of twilight. This may in some cases be catastrophic for the atmosphere of the planet – if the difference between the day and nightside is severe enough and the nightside is cold enough, the atmosphere can freeze out on the nightside. However, since the first discoveries of habitable zone planets, most of which are likely tidally locked, modelling efforts have demonstrated that atmospheric circulation in these bodies is likely sufficient to keep the atmosphere at a (relatively) stable temperature throughout the planet and prevent it from evaporating away or freezing out [2, 14-16]. Still, one could imagine some cases where only the small twilight band between the day and nightsides would be truly habitable. Note that on the parts of the planet where Proxima Centauri (the star) is visible, it will be dimmer, redder, but appear three times larger in the sky than the Sun in ours [1]. Alpha Centauri A and B will also be visible in the dayside sky.

Tidal locking may pose some problems for retaining an atmosphere, but a much more severe threat to the habitability of planets around low-mass stars is the high magnetic and X-ray activity of these stars. For our own Sun, this activity produces solar flares as well as coronal mass ejections (where chunks of gas from the corona, the outer atmosphere of the Sun, actually can be flung towards the Earth), which can impact power grids and electronics here on Earth. In March 1989, a coronal mass ejection struck the Earth, producing extremely intense aurorae visible as far south as Texas and Florida in the USA – and knocking out power to Quebec, Canada for 9 hours. An even stronger coronal mass ejection hit the Earth during the Carrington event of 1859, when extraordinarily bright aurorae were observed worldwide. Reportedly, the aurorae were so bright, it was possible to read the newspaper by aurora-light alone! This geomagnetic disturbance caused telegraph systems in Europe and North America to fail, even giving some telegraph operators electronic shocks. This would be calamitous in today's electronically-connected world, knocking out electronics, mobile grids, the internet, etc. – some estimates suggest it could take several years to recover from such an event.

Low-mass stars are much more active than the Sun, producing frequent strong flares and coronal mass ejections, and Proxima Centauri is no exception. Recently, Howard et al. 2018 [8] detected a "superflare" from this star, significantly stronger than solar flares, and several other high-energy flares over their multi-year observation campaign. While such superflares may have produced amazing auroral displays, this is not good news for habitability. With this level of activity, Proxima Centauri b likely would have lost its protective ozone layer very quickly, allowing sterilising UV radiation through to the surface of this planet [8]. Ribas et al. 2016 [15] estimate that Proxima Centauri b receives 30 times more extreme-UV and 250 times more X-ray radiation than the Earth. This would kill most simple bacteria; thus, if life exists on Proxima Centauri b, it must have evolved significant defences to this extreme radiation environment.

Size and, more importantly, composition and density can also play a large role in planet habitability. The Earth is a rocky planet – the oceans and atmosphere are only a very thin fluid layer over an almost altogether rocky planet. For life (as we know it, at least) to be present requires liquid water to be present; thus, a planet that is mostly gaseous (for instance, a habitable zone analogue of Neptune) is unlikely to host life, as there is no rocky surface for water to collect on. A waterworld planet that is 100% ocean without any rocky surface, surprisingly, may also be a difficult place for life to evolve. The bottom of such an ocean would be composed of high-pressure ices; at very high pressures, the resulting extreme compression will cause water to form ices at temperatures considerably above the freezing point temperature of water at 1 bar [5]. Recently, Kite & Ford 2018 [10] have argued that in some cases, however, a waterworld could be habitable for a few billion years of its total lifetime.

3. How to determine if a planet is actually habitable

To determine if planets such as Proxima Centauri b and the TRAPPIST-1 planets are truly habitable, we must detect light directly from the atmosphere of the planet itself. With light collected over a wide range of wavelengths using a spectrometer, we can search for biosignatures that might be indicative of the presence of life. A number of potential biosignatures have been proposed, including the signature of vegetation on a planet's surface (the "red edge" [17]) and the simultaneous presence of spectral absorption features from oxygen, methane, and ozone in the same atmosphere [12]. Next-generation telescopes, both on the ground and in space, will begin to allow us to access biosignatures in the spectra of habitable zone planets around low-mass stars, giving us our first indication as to whether they are truly habitable.

Spectra for the TRAPPIST-1 planets, which transit their star, can be reconstructed via measuring the depth of the transit at different wavelengths. At a wavelength where there is more absorption in the atmosphere, the planet will appear bigger, as a photon at this wavelength from its star will not be able to penetrate as deeply into the atmosphere before being absorbed, compared to a photon at a wavelength with less absorption. Thus, the planet will appear somewhat larger or somewhat smaller at different wavelengths, depending on absorption at these wavelengths, and produce a deeper or shallower transit respectively. The first spectra acquired for 4 of the 7 TRAPPIST-1 planets using this method with the Hubble Space Telescope [4] are very low resolution – these spectra rule out cloud-free puffy, hydrogen-dominated atmospheres for 3 of these 4 planets, but multiple atmospheric models still fit the data within the reported errors and the resolution obtained is too low to retrieve details about specific gas spectral features in this atmosphere. The James Webb Space Telescope (henceforth JWST) will yield much higher-precision spectra for the TRAPPIST-1 planets. Krissansen-Totton et al. 2018 [12] suggest that JWST observations may be able to detect biogenic gases such as methane and CO in the atmosphere of TRAPPIST-1e.

To date, no transit has been measured for Proxima Centauri b, thus measuring spectra during a transit is not possible for this planet. However, JWST observations may be able to determine if Proxima Centauri b has an atmosphere or not [11]. Since Proxima Centauri b is tidally locked, it may have a significant temperature difference between the irradiated dayside and the cooler nightside. Over the 11 day orbital period of the planet, different fractions of the dayside will be visible from the Earth. With a very sensitive instrument working at mid-infrared wavelengths (such as the Mid-IR Instrument on JWST), this will result in a slight brightening in the unresolved light of the combined planet+star system when a higher fraction of the dayside is visible from Earth compared to when the nightside is primarily visible. Thus, the amplitude of the variation when the nightside is visible vs. when the dayside is visible will give an indication of the temperature difference between the two sides of the planet. This would be similar to measuring the brightness of the full moon versus the brightness of the new moon, in order to measure the temperature difference between the dayside and nightside of the moon. A large variation (similar to what you would find for the Moon) would indicate a rocky planet without an atmosphere, where the dayside is heated to a much higher temperature than the nightside, while a small variation would indicate the presence of an atmosphere, where atmospheric circulation prevents the difference in temperature between the dayside and the nightside from becoming very large.

To yield spectra of Proxima Centauri b will entail actually imaging the planet – in other words, producing a resolved image of the planet orbiting its star. To date, 10 planets have been imaged around other stars (see, e.g. [3, 13]). The planets imaged to date are much more massive, hotter, and younger than Proxima Centauri b. They are analogues to Jupiter in our own Solar System, but imaged at a very young age (100 million years old, which is really only young in the astronomical context). At these young ages, they are still contracting and cooling and are much hotter than planets in our own Solar System, which have had about 5 billion years to cool off. This class of exoplanet have temperatures around 800 degrees Celsius, comparable to the temperature of a candle flame! Thus, they are much brighter in the infrared than they will be when they reach ages similar to our own solar system, and thus comparatively easier to image.

In comparison, Proxima Centauri has an age similar to the Sun, so any planets in the system would have had plenty of time to cool. Proxima Centauri b is a lot smaller and cooler, and hence much fainter than the planets imaged to date. A 30–40 m diameter telescope is necessary to reach the resolutions and contrasts to potentially image this planet. Luckily, three such extremely large telescopes (henceforth ELTs) will be coming online in the next decade! However, while ELTs may image Proxima Centauri b, they may not be able to deliver spectra with suitable spectral resolution to robustly detect biosignatures – this may need to wait for dedicated space missions in the 2030s, such as the planned LUVOIR mission (an acronym which creatively stands for Large UV Optical Infrared Telescope). Nonetheless, in the next decade, our understanding of the atmospheres (or lack thereof) of habitable zone exoplanets will be transformed by the combination of JWST and ELTs, and we will be able to make our first steps at least towards determining whether these planets are truly habitable or even inhabited.

One hundred years from now, I personally suspect that we will have detected non-terrestrial life, either on one of the frozen water-ice moons of our Solar System or via spectral signatures in an atmosphere of an Earth-like planet orbiting another star. However, the most likely scenario is that the first non-terrestrial life we find will be relatively simple, akin to microbes. Finding civilisations like our own is considerably more difficult – and probably requires such a civilisation to wish to be found. Ultimately, it seems unlikely that Proxima Centauri b would host an advanced civilisation, but for now it is certainly fun to speculate.

References

[1] G. Anglada-Escudé et al. A terrestrial planet candidate in a temperate orbit around Proxima Centauri. *Nature*, 536:437-440, August 2016.

[2] R. Barnes et al. The Habitability of Proxima Centauri b I: Evolutionary Scenarios. *ArXiV e-prints.*

[3] G. Chauvin et al. Discovery of a warm, dusty giant planet around HIP 65426. *Astron. & Astrophys.*, 605-L9, September 2017.

[4] J. de Wit et al. Atmospheric reconnaissance of the habitable-zone Earth-sized planets orbiting TRAPPIST-1. *Nature Astronomy*, 2:21-219, March 2018.

[5] D. H. Dolan, M. D. Knudson, C. A. Hall, and C. Deeney. A metastable limit for compressed liquid water. *Nature Physics*, 3:339-342, May 2007.

[6] M. Gillon et al. Seven temperate terrestrial planets around the nearby ultracool dwarf star TRAPPIST-1. *Nature*, 542:456-460, February 2017.

[7] S. L. Grimm et al. The nature of the TRAPPIST-1 exoplanets. *Astron.*

& *Astrophys.*, 613:A68, June 2018.

[8] W. S. Howard et al. The First Naked-eye Superflare Detected from Proxima Centauri. *Astrophys. J. Lett.*, 860:L30, June 2018.

[9] J. F. Kasting and D. Catling. Evolution of a Habitable Planet. *Ann. Rev. of Astron. & Astrophys.*, 41:429-463, 2003.

[10] E. S. Kite and E. B. Ford. Habitability of Exoplanet Waterworlds. *Astro-phys. J*, 864:75, September 2018.

[11] L. Kreidberg and A. Loeb. Prospects for Characterizing the Atmosphere of Proxima Centauri b. *Astrophys. J. Lett.*, 832:L12, November 2016.

[12] J. Krissansen-Totton, R. Garland, P. Irwin, and D. C. Catling. Detectability of Biosignatures in Anoxic Atmospheres with the James Webb Space Telescope: A TRAPPIST-1e Case Study. *Astron. J.*, 156:114, September 2018.

[13] B. Macintosh et al. Discovery and spectroscopy of the young jovian planet 51 Eri b with the Gemini Planet Imager. *Science*, 350:64-67, October 2015.

[14] V. S. Meadows et al. The Habitability of Proxima Centauri b: Environmental States and Observational Discriminants. *Astrobiology*, 18:133-189, February 2018.

[15] I. Ribas et al. The habitability of Proxima Centauri b. I. Irradiation, rotation and volatile inventory from formation to the present. *Astron. & Astrophys.*, 596:A111, December 2016.

[16] M. Turbet et al. The habitability of Proxima Centauri b. II. Possible climates and observability. *Astron. & Astrophys.*, 596:A112, December 2016.

[17] N. J. Woolf, P. S. Smith, W. A. Traub, and K. W. Jucks. The Spectrum of Earthshine: A Pale Blue Dot Observed from the Ground. *Astrophys. J*, 574:430-433, July 2002.

Tacye Phillipson is Senior Curator of Science at National Museums Scotland. She was lead curator for the Enquire gallery, which looks at how scientists have sought to answer questions, and the many different aspects of science. She has previously curated exhibitions on topics from prosthetic limbs to Napier's rods and the Higgs boson.

Alien collecting: speculative museology

Tacye Phillipson

When we visit some place new, we often wish to acquire souvenirs to remind us of our travels and show off on our return. It is possible that, as well as making observations of Earth and eventually inviting humans to Proxima Centauri b, the aliens would have collected items – for later study, to display in their equivalent of a museum or possibly as personal souvenirs. But what might have been taken back from Scotland?

Humanity's extra-terrestrial collecting so far has only extended to rocks and dust – mainly from the lunar missions. However, there simply weren't any other items to collect, and much greater choice would face our aliens in their visits to Earth. The decisions the aliens would need to make about what to take back have similarities to the choices that face both museums nowadays and collectors on past voyages of exploration, study and acquisition. By considering some of the collecting done by humans, we can speculate about potential alien collecting.

When considering collecting new material for National Museums Scotland, I can only acquire a minute fraction of everything that is possible. With relatively modern material I know that I am often condemning the item to be scrapped or recycled when I do not take it in to the museum collections. Other objects we believe will remain valued outside the museum. Some of the things collected in the past have, during their centuries of preservation in collections, changed from being ordinary and common to special and noteworthy survivals, or indeed from being of current major significance to an obscure historical object. Likewise, extra-terrestrial visitors could only collect a tiny proportion of all the things in Scotland, and some of the material a long lived alien might collect when it was common would become rare or even unique in the universe in future.

Why are items being collected?

What might the alien's motivation be behind collecting objects? A scholarly expedition is likely to gather material relating to the topic of research for further study; material with details or significance that images, descriptions and other such surrogates for the object itself cannot fully capture. Some material will find future academic use which is not initially thought of by the collectors. An example of this is DNA research on specimens collected before DNA was even discovered. Of course, anything might conceivably be interesting in future for a currently unimagined project, and it is impossible to collect or preserve everything. A common guide is to prioritise material which has a current purpose.

As well as study, another use for material is display, either informally as souvenirs or to present as exhibitions and to disseminate the results of the research trip. That an audience attended the performance in this story, 'A Certain Reverence' implies an interest in humans which might well have extended to other specimens from Earth. A significant audience for this sort of exhibition are the funders – we have no idea how the aliens organise and resource their expeditions, but would there be significant stakeholders who wanted to see, or even acquire, items from Earth? One trip might acquire several examples of something to distribute to interested parties and supporters.

It is hard to know what an alien might find worthy of study or display. They would probably be unimpressed by anything which related to the laws of physics and chemistry or a technology any advanced civilisation could master. But things that relate to the choices humans make might be much more interesting and uniquely human. Clothing is one item that might well have been collected – it has such a huge variety of aspects of personal choice and societal invention. Both the completed articles of clothing and the fabric they are made from are uniquely human. Tartan might well feature for any alien interested in Scotland, depending on when in history they visited. Handmade lace might be particularly fascinating because of its complicated and hugely labour intensive nature. The over and under of relatively simple weaving might be invented many times but lace techniques seem more likely to be unique.

Practical considerations

There is usually some limitation on size of objects to be collected, whether weight or volume. While the spaceship or museum stores may be large, they are never large enough to contain everything, so a lot will need to be left uncollected and unrepresented in the collection. The six Apollo missions to the Moon brought back a total of 382kg of rock, sand and dust, but they could not collect and transport everything of potential interest. Hundreds of tiny items can be packed into the same space taken up by one large one, but smallness isn't everything. Larger items may be wanted despite or even because of their size: a Moon rock may be more interesting than more grains of Moon sand. It is also much less useful to collect items if you don't know much about them or can't fully record when and where they came from. Collecting lots of smaller individual objects will often need far more work and time to document and pack than a single larger item, but a linked group of items can show more than a single example. Sometimes a smaller part of something will be collected to represent the whole, such as a spare rivet from the Forth Bridge.

When considering what to collect, the material and how long it will last are important. Purely from the preservation point of view, Haggis may not be the best choice for a souvenir to collect in Scotland. While the Edinburgh Museum of Science and Art did collect a number of examples of food stuffs in the 1860s, this did not prove to be a good long-term idea for the collection. Many of these samples decayed and had to be withdrawn from the collection by the 1880s. It isn't only food and organic materials which may not prove to be a good long-term choice for preservation. As materials are intentionally made to biodegrade and cause minimum harm to the environment, additional challenges for long-term preservation are created.

What might an alien collect?

Aliens would probably not see elements or simple compounds like gold or rubies as worth collecting, as they will occur in many other places in the galaxy. But many minerals and rocks show the effects of life, from the effects of atmospheric oxygen to fossils. Limestone, which is formed from the remains of sea creatures, and marble (metamorphised limestone) may be unique to Earth. Scottish midges, grass and moss might be of interest – common here, but unique to Earth. But would they be collected as living and animate organisms or as fixed and dead specimens? A scientifically advanced and long-lived alien would be very aware of the evolutionary changes to be expected within a small captive population, compared to the larger wild gene pool, so perhaps they would collect in both ways.

These are all natural materials. Would the aliens see human-made items as more special than, say, a bird's nest? Possibly they would, because of the great variety of things made by humans, but they might not share our assessment of what is most significant and worth collecting. Often a collector's assessment is different from the creator's. A collector in a new area or culture may be interested more in what is characteristic and common than the outliers and unusual, which gain their significance from comparison with the more normal.

Would an alien want to collect a mobile phone? They are a common and significant part of human culture and an example of the capabilities of our technology and design choices. However, they are only a lump of material when switched off or unconnected, and there won't be much chance of getting a signal on Proxima Centauri b. A phone might be collected as representative of the whole information technology industry and network. If it were intended to be kept for a long time and maybe studied later, then the aliens would need to be concerned with the varied ways in which it might degrade. Storing batteries in good condition for decades is a problem, and plastics can go brittle or sticky over time.

We know these aliens are fascinated with bagpipes, but like the mobile phone a bagpipe without its player is a very different and literally deflated object. I am sure they could build a bagpipe-playing robot to inflate and squeeze the bag and cover the finger holes should they wish to, but then they would also need to maintain the bagpipe and its reeds in working order. Perhaps recordings would be a favoured option for them to collect, with better ability to be preserved for the long term than a working bagpipe. This could be combined with an example of an instrument preserved for examination or display, but not to be continuously maintained in working order, with the necessary repairs and loss of its original nature and without the human artistry of the player.

The aliens might also consider the ethics of what they are collecting – is it right to remove and permanently deprive the planet Earth of the item? Or of anything at all? Before the aliens had announced themselves, they could not ask full permission, though they could have portrayed themselves as planning to take the items to a foreign country. Would this affect what was collected, perhaps directing it towards items seen as more ordinary by people, but still special to the aliens? Or material that was in the process of being lost or destroyed, such as items on a sinking ship? This also raises the question about return of items. If the aliens, during their long study of Earth, had collected something like Pictish clothing and preserved it in pristine condition it would over time become hugely significant for humans in a way it had not been originally. Might the aliens feel obliged to consider its return, and if so when? Or might they not mention it, to avoid interfering with the natural course of history, forgetting, and archaeology?

Collecting people?

In inviting humans to visit Proxima Centauri b and perform there, our aliens have demonstrated behaviour that we can recognise in humans. We too invite and welcome performers from around the globe to visit Edinburgh during the festival and admire different performances and cultures. Historically, intrepid travellers from far countries have been welcomed with fascination, such as Ahutoru, the first Tahitian to visit Europe. Less comfortably for modern sensibilities, human zoos and freakshows once welcomed, persuaded and forced people to travel and present versions of their life as performances to the curious. In this story, were Blair and her companions willing explorers and adventurers seizing a great opportunity, or were they being taken advantage of? Or both? Alien reasoning and ethical standards have no reason to be similar to our own current ones. What might astro-sociologists deduce about the aliens' ethics from this invitation to *perform*? Were human beings being 'collected' like souvenirs or specimens?

Scotland
at the end of the Universe

Russell Jones is a writer and editor. He's published 5 poetry collections, plus short stories for adults and children. Russell has edited 3 writing anthologies and is deputy editor of *Shoreline of Infinity*, a sci-fi magazine. He is the UK's first Pet Poet Laureate and has a PhD in Creative Writing.

Far

Russell Jones

***

we reminisce through photographs

***

I remember it like it was tomorrow – we met 6 degrees North of midnight, The Royal Observatory, Edinburgh; your eye was on the chronoscope I'd waited months to use.

"We can share," I said. You were much too brilliant to argue with, I knew I'd lose

myself in your eyes, your pupils like black holes.

a laugh like glass

like kittens in boxes

like light

stretched across a great expanse

I wouldn't call it love at first sight, because I think you were cautious at first, maybe even irritated. But it was enough. We discussed our work – you pretended to be impressed with me, I really was impressed with you. You were too smart, too suave-nerd, too good-looking and socially-acceptable for someone like me, I thought.

Then we drank at *The World's End.*

"So, *you're* the other chronotopographer in Scotland. I thought we'd never meet," you half-joke. Soon, your hand touches mine and we pretend it's an accident. "My round. Shots?"

You'll make me forget myself, but I nod. You're impressively quick, nauseatingly generous:

we drink

    and drink

        and drink

           each other in.

The last shot took my breath, and I must have turned pale.

"Close your eyes. Breathe," I heard you say. "Just breathe."

I obeyed.

I was quiet then, rarely went out (except to work) because I didn't have much to go out for. You started slowly: movies, meals at home, quiet restaurants. Then games nights with your close friends, camping just outside the city borders (when the heat and smog were safe). Eventually we flew to Paris and Madrid. By the end of it, I probably wouldn't have recognised myself.

And it feels like the years passed without us noticing. We mapped time like we map our lives: a sequence of bubbles and lines we could comprehend, hanging them around our flat like artwork:

The lounge   The hallway   The kitchen

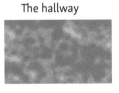

We exchange keys, hips, data, lips. Our lives converge: two adjacent lines reaching out until they appear as one, bold and straight. Once altered, there's no reversal, is there? I hope not, I can't go back now.

We'll talk about time, children and retirement. We'll maybe even buy a campervan so we can visit the clear and clean spaces to watch the sky, sheep like dandelion clocks, and I can't wait.

Then that letter arrives...

"I've been offered a job. A really good one. I didn't even apply," you will say, twiddling your hair in that way which (I'll learn) will tell me you're nervously excited, or excitedly nervous.

"Where?"

"England."

The thing about inflation is, it's hard to stop: the balloon fattens until it bursts; the lung swells to an ached exhale; we grow happy, then happier, and then you're gone. The universe won't simply obey us, it needs a pin prick or a fist in its face, a sudden jolt to stop.

And so that's where we stopped: we sold the flat to pay for your move, loaded the lorry with pieces of you, filled our diaries to stay busy.

I felt the knife cut, our line fork.

Of course, we will tell ourselves

IT'S OKAY

(A lot of couples go through this, we'll persist, we'll outlive this flicker. Our lives aren't linear, we can cope with change and – in a sense – we will never not be together... right?)

Monday	Tuesday	Wednesday	Thursday	Friday	Saturday	Sunday
28	29	30	31	1 Feb	2	3
work						
4	5	6	7	8	9	10
wait						

Three months are lost. You said they'd fly by, but I felt each hour weigh me down. I feel my old self creeping back in, like a butterfly returning to its cocoon. I watch TV alone, buy takeaways to avoid having to go out, waiting for your messages to arrive. And when they do, I analyse every word as though it's corrupted data, trying to pick out the anomalies. And I watch the clocks until

you visited. We ate at our favourite old haunt, testing our favourite dishes for change (You: haggis bon bons with raspberry jam, despite the pretention. Me: pie, despite my anxiety).

"How's it going down there?" I asked, trying to extract hidden truths from you.

You practically glow. I feel sick. "It's a great set-up, we're reaching out further than ever, finding new pockets of dark matter, new voids and compressions we could never find with our old tech."

Your giddiness stings me. I wanted you to be (at least a bit)

miserable,

to see our future

up here, together,

where our foundations lie.

"You'll have to visit soon," you say. "The air's hot and heavy, but England's really not so bad."

And then I realise that we've become Visitors.

I think you sense that worry in me, because you quickly pay the bill, take my hand and lead me outside.

"We're going back," you say, sternly. I like that, it feels like you again. I want you to take control. "Come on, let's walk."

We pass through the drowsy city, its bars yawning, curtains closing, cars sleeping on driveways, up the steep dark hill to the observatory. We ascend to the chronoscopes, where we first met.

You will adjust the lenses with such tender precision that I'll become jealous. I want to be those lenses, for you to see through my eyes, to have your fingers on my skin again. You'll tell me to look now, ask if I notice anything special.

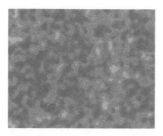

"No, just clumps of dark matter, it's quite dense."

"Keep looking. I was leading a seminar last week, and I realised: so many people think maps are about showing truth, but they only show an angle." I don't move as you load a filter. "Look again."

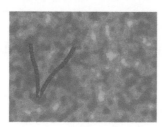

"Vee?"

"That's you," you said.

You step in behind me, arms wrapped around my waist, so close I feel your breath on the back of my neck. You take my hand and pull my strings, adjusting the lenses through my fingers.

"And here's me."

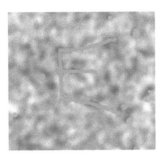

"You've been busy." I almost laugh but don't want to seem cruel or unimpressed. I love that you can find meaning in the darkest places.

"I like my work," you say. "But I miss you, you idiot." You pull me away and kiss me and my worries start to dissolve, my wings start to flutter. "Every time I look out, even in the data, I still see you. You're starting to skew my results."

"Sorry."

We sneak into the planetarium, mostly used for kids' visits, and lie on the soda-stained carpet, staring up at the stars and comets together, and – despite my hesitations – I feel like our lines have merged again.

***

see the sun in each other's eyes

***

The cobbled streets are pulsing with drums and bagpipes, light beams and lanterns, cheers erupting from dark alleys and high windows. I am happily anonymous here, amongst thousands of revellers, some wearing painted or plastic masks, the mirrored sky still hot on our faces.

Yes

this is what you wanted. Scotland will cauterise itself from the hobbling foot.

Yes

I can imagine the spark in your eyes, your hair like wildfire when we dance and drink.

Yes

our dreams will return with you. I've already found the perfect campervan and scopes, a loan we can afford to repay. I wish I could weave this future into a reality.

"I can't wait," you say, calling, "I miss you, and home."

"Things will be different once Scotland's on the other side of the universe."

You laugh. "No shit, Sherlock. Have a good night, tonight. You won't get too wrecked, will you?"

"No promises. Are you celebrating?"

"Maybe just a little. You know, the usual."

We both go out to celebrate with colleagues, our borders weakening. I go to *The World's End* and send you a photo of my order at the bar:

Quick as an Inflation Drive, you send a photo back:

So, we're both in for a heavy night. I smile to myself.

My colleagues chat about the next jump. There will be a final trial of the Inflation Drive before Scotland separates far across the universe permanently, now the vote and die has been cast. A new star for our new nation, no more hot air from politicians and mirrored skies.

"A truly independent Scotland will manage its own policies, as decided by the people," the First Minister broadcasts, and the people in the pub are silent as they watch. "We will be a healthier, happier nation. This is a momentous time in our nation's history."

The pub roars, people dance and empty their merry drinks merrily. A woman in a blue dress asks me if I'd like to dance, probably because I'm sat alone and look bored or sad, but I shake my head. Dancing makes my blood itch and legs warble.

Do you remember the ceilidh when I faltered so horribly through Strip the Willow that the band had to stop playing? I'm convinced we were invited to fewer weddings after that.

I stumble towards home now, the booze ripe in my veins, Princes Street intoxicated with songs and flags, its air purity sensors winking safe-green. If I were to map this moment, in this space, how might it look? The energy, the hope – maybe they would emit a yellow-orange tint, like a rising sun. I need a pint of Irn-Bru and a pizza crunch. I unwillingly return the high-fives of a group of party-goers as they pass, then pick up my pace.

Almost home now, just past the stadium and the memory store, two patrons sway outside a pub, swathed in the separation flags:

"Sixth jump's the charm!" one says.

"Think we'll make the cut, for good?"

"That's what they say. Can't trust a politician though, can ya?"

They eye me as I approach, nod and smile. "Alright pal."

"Alright."

"Have a good'un."

"You too, pal."

Home, I push my finger against the pad and climb the stairs. Sixth jump's the charm. You'll be back here/there for the seventh. Not long now, we can be ourselves again.

***

we stretch our arms out, make telescopes

***

The butterfly emerges, spreads its new wings: the left tip unfolds from the right.

At one tip of the universe,   Far far away, further than I can
England crisps   possibly comprehend, Scotland
under the old sun.   hatches anew, with everyone intact,
                                               gazing at the unfamiliar sky.

((The Inflation Drive hibernates until it's primed to return us))

I create maps as quickly as I can, helping our scouts to evade dark matter clusters or voids, so we can properly survey the time and space between us. We'll return to restock, make sure everyone's in their place, before the final jump.

Between work and coffee, I research our possibilities and find a cosy hillside just north of Edinburgh for our first weekend reunited, a little cottage-stay

where they will serve shortbread and scones,

where we will look out at this far-flung side of our universe

through new lenses.

I can't wait for you to see what we have made (could make) here, to unfurl our wings and plot new maps together.

I take a break and climb to the sky deck. I look through the curved glass, out over the city; I imagine myself gliding over the roofs and spires, looking down on our favourite spaces, each filled with our memories despite them being so far from you. Edinburgh looks no different, except that the closest star is low in the sky, warming us rather than roasting us. The air is cooler without the mirrored skies, children play in the park now, adults stroll to work, maskless, but otherwise everything is strangely similar. The separation feels healthy, natural. A flock of ducks passes over, landing in the trench of a dry loch. When the loch has been refilled, let's visit them with loaves of bread.

I could stay up here for hours, thinking of you.

But I have to work quickly: I start to thread data back towards Earth, using my dark matter maps to navigate through speed-ports and around time-sinks, following the paths of least resistance to make the data's journey smoother. Although the ID can move us physically in an instant when required, the routes for our transmissions are still horribly slow. It will take years of research and teamwork to straighten out.

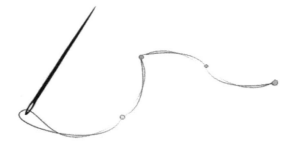

Life might be tough for a while – all new beginnings have their challenges, but this place promises us something we could never have back there: change.

The observatory looks the same, but it feels different. Sometimes, when the instruments creak, I think I hear you. Sometimes, just as I'm about to fall asleep, I feel you lying next to me. I stay busy, wishing our return time was shorter, ready for our final jump together.

I forget when the message arrives from the Head of Department. It was dark, I was sleeping. But it arrives...

```
Inflation Drive must stay offline.

Temporary ID ban.

Need SDOS response, ASAP.

What do we say?
```

The news will spread fast across the country. Scotland here, everyone else over there.

You and I will be apart. Families will be parted, trades severed

and yet there will be some jubilation: "This was the plan anyway, wasn't it?" a few will say, "To be separate, independent!"

But most will curse the politicians for their mistakes, as I did. Without the Inflation Drive to return, we are, were, will be

deserted.

I cluster with my colleagues in the meeting room. The coffee-breath tells me nobody's slept.

"I've got kids, I need to get back!" the Deputy Programmer snaps. "They can't do this!"

"My partner's sick, who'll take care of them?" our PhD Student groans, holding back tears. "What's going on?"

"Everyone, please, I'll tell you what I know," the Head of Department says. "My kid's getting married in a month, I don't want to miss it either."

"A MONTH?!" the room shudders.

I feel their panic too, like a taut rope is about to be cut. Trial jumps normally last just a few days.

"It probably won't be that long," the Head of Department says. "Data's coming through very slowly – their message was probably sent as soon as we jumped here. It looks like there's been a ban imposed on ID travel. The drive's causing anomalies."

"Like what?" the Deputy Programmer asks.

"We don't know that yet, we'll have to wait for more information."

The PhD Student wipes their eyes on their sleeve. "So, we're stranded?"

"We'll carry on as usual and wait for the ban to be lifted."

"But we could go back if we wanted to?" I pipe up.

"No."

"Is the ID broken?"

"No, but—"

"—so we can use it anyway. We don't need to do as we're told by UDOS now."

"We've tried, their ID isn't responding."

"They've turned it off!" the Deputy Programmer shrieks. "They've left us here!"

The room erupts in bawls and curses.

"We don't know that," the Head of Department growls. "Either way, we can't risk causing unknown damage. Unsanctioned use of the ID could hurt people back home, or worse. Folks, let's just be patient. We wait for information, this could all be over in a day or so. We keep working, as usual, prioritising communications through Chrononavigation – am I understood?" They stare at me.

We all nod and murmur, "Yes."

"Thank you. Now, back to work."

I return to my station and sink into my seat, a question repeating and repeating in my mind:

What if I never see you again?

***

not everything is lost in a failed flight.

***

4 days

One day – it must be early summer, because we are sat on the grass – you made us daisy chain crowns and bracelets. I've been holding this ring in my pocket for weeks, but every opportunity has felt forced. My time's running out, and the question sits in my gut.

"You are the daisy-god, what will you say to your beloved worshippers?" you ask, with that goofy kid grin you have, rows of daisies bowing their heads in prayer before me. I must look serious, because you adjust your crown. "You okay?"

I reached into my pocket and felt for the box. It's just a loop of metal, a jewel, just a promise. You'll be in England soon, I don't know how we'll continue but this could help bind us.

"Yeh, it's nothing," I say, smiling as I drop the ring into my pocket again. "I shall tell my worshippers that they are loved, and to bring me sandwiches."

"Soppy git!" You eat crisps. A dog licks your fingers and you laugh; you tell their owner it's okay.

This is what we should be doing forever, isn't it?

What are you doing now?

11	12	13	14	15	16	17
look for me						

18	19	20	21	22	23	24
		look for me	please			don't give up

Work is painful and slow. My maps are like matches burning in a dark room. After work, we're all too tired to pretend things are fine or that progress has been made. We sit in cafes and bars, avoiding journalists and listening to people talk – the way frightened kids listen to their parents argue through closed doors or floorboards.

Nobody wants to admit this, but we don't know what to do. We're angry and afraid, and we're not used to not knowing.

***
eclipse
***

1.5 weeks

There are whispers inside whispers...

we've been quarantined
we've been lost
the earth's lost
the earth's at war
warnings came in
instead
of answers
of annihilation we cut off
we cut
we were an experiment
an experiment gone
wrong
wrong coordinates
wrong space
wrong time
time will forget us
punish us
we are being punished because
because of the vote
because of the ID
the ID
creates instability the ID
creates uncertainty the ID
creates possibilities the ID
creates

These rumours fall like snow. Every time we step outside, they land on our shoulders, and I shiver as I feel them layering into something impenetrable. The media's turned (predictably) cold and feral, protestors drum the streets into submission, parliament does what little it can to blanket our fears, but there is nothing new or reassuring to say.

"Remain calm, we have our best people working on it," they told people. And it works. But there will be a moment when it won't work anymore and the gates will be breached. They will blame us.

I am given the time and protection I need to toil at my maps, using arrays and scopes to improve them each day, to stretch my hand slowly towards you. Data trickles through, sluggish and scrambled, like it's been wading through a storm.

There are two streams of data coming in:

1) An official stream, encrypted. Without the passcodes, they mean nothing to me, so I send them to my Head of Department.

2) Dozens of our map references (this is your doing, isn't it?). I check the references against the maps we created together, our secret stash:

Are you trying to show me a path or pattern? I'm sorry, I don't see it.

I spend an entire night looking at the codes of map references on repeat, muddled and reordered – it must be some mistake, a data echo caused by the journey through troublesome time-sinks and speed-ports.

And so I scoop up the data and present it to our Head of Department.

"Is this it?" They almost spit coffee.

"It's horribly slow," I explain. "The routes are long and we can't avoid the time dilations yet. It'll take years to—"

"—Keep working on the data routes back, we need more than numbers," they tell me, and I agree. I look for quick routes through the time dilations, using dark matter clusters and voids as my Sherpas and horses.

You're much better at this than I am.
You'd be staunch, stoic, a rock.

But I'm a mess, barely sleeping, barely
able to calculate the most familiar figures
and faces.

You'd see something I haven't. You'd find some way
to bring us back until
we're prepared to return.

(Will that day ever come, now?)
I'm out of ideas, can you lend me one?

The team will hold more pointless meetings where we argue, and I'll watch my colleagues worn thin with fatigue and worry. I can see the PhD Student's about to crumble; the same erosion's beginning in myself and others, each of us desperate not to tumble into the black voids around us.

Afterwards I walk to the sky deck to settle myself. I look for ducks again, but see none. People are gathered in clumps in the streets below, and I'm glad that they're not at our gates. The tethers of society are fraying and I predict the tension's about to make us snap. Last night, someone sprayed the observatory visitor centre with a doomsday clock and red paint graffito: *your fault.*

The PhD Student is here too, staring across Edinburgh as if haunted. They smile weakly and – despite my intuition, or maybe because of it – I approach.

"What a mess," they say.

"How are you doing?"

They look at me with a hint of disdain, then soften. "I just want to know my partner's okay. I want to be there for them. What if they're gone already and I didn't see them?"

"I know." What we needed then was hope, I thought. I don't have facts, but a lie holds power in its roots. "We'll get back, I know we will."

"How?"

I force a smile. "Well, I don't know *that* yet." The sky deck rotates slowly and the Scott Monument slides into view, spearing the sky. "But our team's smart, we're resilient. We're not going to give up. And who knows, tomorrow the ban could be lifted."

"Yeah, maybe."

It hasn't worked. I've never been one for locker-room talk and morale-boosts, have I? Well, I tried.

"What about you?" the PhD Student asks.

"My partner's back there, too. But I know they're working on getting us back."

"They work in ID?"

I nod. "They're a chronotopographer too. Between us all, we'll fix this. And I'm sure everyone's taking care of your par –"

The door behind us slams open.

"The ban's been lifted!" a colleague yells from the doorway. "We're going home!"

***

in disbelief, we see

***

4 months

No.   Too slow.   Too chaotic.

Maybe...   no. If we can navigate around...   It's just too far.


```
I want to smash these plates, burn
these maps. All the days and hours
I've wept here, I'm starting to see
routes where there are none, starting to lose
you, like hope, in the dark.

- Feeling crap, sometime around midnight
```

It didn't take long for the truth to emerge: the ban hadn't been lifted, the ID signal from Earth was dead. Rumours are a virus here, and it's hard to immunise ourselves against them.

The map references keep seeping in, a little faster and more frequently than before (our routes are improving, aren't they?) but just as pointlessly. The public don't know it yet, but it's been two months since the official encrypted data stopped.

Why are you giving us the silent treatment?

My needle's wearing blunt. My threads are knotted, and the further our tools try to weave, the more difficult the pattern becomes. I wasn't even trying to get us home, a school-kid could tell you it's impossible without the ID, but I wanted to send our voices out to be heard, to have you listen and respond.

And there are a lot of things for you to hear: Parliament has been reopened, just a week since the bombing. The police quickly stopped a spate of lootings which threatened to spread. They are meant to reassure us, fluorescent with their yellow jackets and black scanners (little bees patrolling the hive), but they remind us of what could happen if more bad news were to break.

Some people have been drawn together though, forming support groups, food shares and trauma centres. It's unexpected but encouraging, how society's fixing itself under the duress of this distance. The PhD Student asked if I wanted to see a movie one night, but I stayed here alone to monitor the data streams.

"We need to focus on living," the First Minister said on their broadcast. "Farmers will still grow their crops. Teachers will still teach their pupils. Police Officers will still walk our streets. Politicians will still lead this country. Scientists will still research and revolutionise. We will persist and we will thrive."

And somehow, for now, we have found a way to get on with things.

I escape my lab for some air on the sky deck. I catch the faint scent of cherry blossom on a breeze, and it sends me tumbling back to drinking

you in

under the trees. You were red with the burn of alcohol and sunlight. There were children laughing as they shot each other with water guns and balloons. You asked if I'd ever thought of having kids.

"I've thought about it," I say, pretending I'm funny but avoiding the answer.

"And do you?"

"I'm not sure. We're young."

(What about our careers? Kids would mean there's no going back, wouldn't it?)

"We won't always be."

I was never one for love stories

But you tempted me.

I've been looking at maps for so long that I've forgotten when we are. *Now* seeps into *Then* into *And-Then*. Time and distance feel so malleable and intangible at once, like a string of handkerchiefs pulled from a magician's sleeve.

Am I losing my mind?

"Close your eyes. Breathe," I heard you say. "Just breathe."

I obey.

I exhale slowly and think I am myself again. I try to place our lives in a line, like shot glasses in a bar, setting each date and detail after the next. But how can I be sure all the details are correct? Are your eyes green? I check a photo. Yes. Was our front door black? I've no way to know, and the uncertainty gnaws at me.

What if I forget or taint our lives with some misremembered or imagined detail?

What if I lose us in my fictions?

I don't want you to slip away, not even the smallest memories. I run through them, trying to cling on to each one:

* North Berwick: we were so absorbed in watching the seagulls (so many, how many?) that we didn't notice the dog licking my ice cream. You told their owner it was okay.

* Princes Street Gardens: flower heads bowed in prayer, drumming in the streets, a box squeezed between my fingertips, but it began to rain so we must have gone to *The World's End*.

* The Royal Observatory: I was nervous, you were using the scopes I needed. Your hair was like wildfire, you were much sweeter than I'd expected. We worked together, and you showed me words in the stars.

Is that it?!

I race to unpack our secret stash of maps:

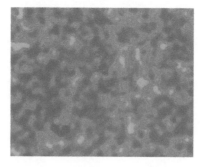

It's been so long that I almost don't see it, but yes, there it is...

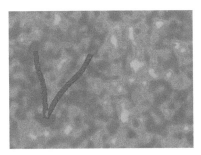

I check the map reference and see it repeat in the data you've been sending, though it's rare. I load more maps, trying to find the other that you showed me, but I've seen so many that it's hard to recall. I sweat and toil for hours, until I find it and highlight you in the clusters:

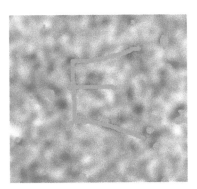

I find the map reference repeating through the data, much more frequently. You sneaky little ferret. I dash to the kitchen, brew a cauldron of coffee and return to the lab.

By the time my colleagues trundle in the next morning, I've cracked your code.

***

spot words in the stars

***

Rukk(Eyo	ojnK)Ftm		oQj3(B2X	5Pt*bs4Q	o}qfUP(E
{NqY]B*K		sDc-c9nz	g8H)tF5L	eMymjheD	
}PRq{q2X	sDc-c9nz	T2UJ]{V6	*BgVQ4Kk	jj}niqD5	f{9cV-7]
Rukk(Eyo	F6Wr7o}m	SGVinRxi	ZxTm5p>5	CLh5LumW	sDc-c9nz
>r{7KCw[	pH5VtBCJ	ed[YQw8S		D(ja>g7o	L4yG(ayr
h8jbax}x	5wX*vSn5	DXTS5PB[		Jop-cagu	{NqY]B*K
	N-6oSNQP	Rukk(Eyo	s-[gCsDG	sDc-c9nz	5wX*vSn5

ID - HEYMANS MULTIV

Inflation Drive - Professor Heymans' chapter on multiverse.

We'd both read those chapters, then dismissed them over a bottle of wine. I load the book, hunting for the relevant passages:

"Much like a toy car rolling down a hill requires a force to stop it, the Inflation Drive causes an expansion so vast and immediate that a huge force must be imparted for the inflation to cease... There are several theories on the possible outcome of stopping the drive, including the creation of alternate universes which co-exist with our own..."

Is this why ID travel has been banned? Are you saying we've been creating universes, or that we've travelled between them? Then maybe the authorities are right, the ID could be too dangerous to use again.

BILD PATH - DNT GIV UP

I've no idea when your messages were sent on their journey, but they arrive a little more quickly with each week that passes. I've a dozen now and, though half of them don't make sense, I know you've been busy building paths to reach me.

But you've used our secret stash of maps to code this. You don't want our messages to be intercepted. Are you okay? What are they doing to you back there?

Please, don't give up. I'm reaching out, too.

V LOVE E

***

and wonder what other worlds there might be

***

7 years

I may not be a genius, but I'm tenacious. My colleagues have been retired or replaced, often convinced we'll never return. Many don't want to get back, they have new lives now, new loves, friends and – in some cases – families. The city whispers as its people move north, tilling the fields and tech farms to feed our different hungers. I have been, am, will be here alone most hours, working, though I hear my colleagues chatter that my department is defunct and should be replaced. So far, my maps are keeping me safe.

For the first few years, we took shifts to test the ID signal, but there was never a response from your side, just the red 'no signal' light pulsing like a wound. Now the ID lies comatose under a white sheet in my lab. Sometimes I dream that the lights flash green, and you appear next to me, but your face is a blur. Sometimes I see you peering into the eyepiece of the chronoscope, or hear your footsteps on the stairs. I'd say this place was haunted, if I believed in ghosts.

Another message arrives and my chest palpitates as I translate it, begging (as I always do) that this isn't the final note I'll receive from you. I almost can't believe

you kept trying all this time.   I'm not

worth it.

found smthng. tell me ASAP if u get this X

I respond with the date, time and my message: Got it. OK?
It's such a cruel tease, but our years of path-finding mean I'll only

have to wait a day or two for a sentence to arrive, rather than weeks. I will busy myself building the bridge, finding intricate twists and turns in my threads back to you.

But tonight I will be sleepless, worrying about what's to follow.

I opened a can of beer, lay on my sleeping bag and looked up at the curved dome ceiling, my instruments glistening. Another message arrived:

```
sos they r onto us radio silence sorry I love
you whatevr hpns remember XXX
```

My hands shake, my fingers were wet and vision blurred as I type my reply: `ru ok? Wht hpnd?`

Nothing. I can't bear the weight of sitting here, not knowing what they had done to you, and I was useless to help.

I type again: `ru ok?`

I thrash through the lab, looking for some device, a hint, a magic wand, a book that could help, but I know there's nothing.

I type: `plz dnt hurt i wl stop`

There's no reply, there won't be for at least a day.

I fall to my sleeping bag, hold it and beg every god I can name, but no more messages arrive, and I feel like I've been emptied, as if every hope and particle of me has been replaced with darkness, and I lie there here and I will am have choked with tears until I slip into a dreamless void of sleep.

*

"Doctor," my Head of Department says, nudging me awake. "You shouldn't sleep in here, I've told you before."

I drag myself up. "Sorry."

"I'm sorry." They pull out my chair and motion for me to sit. "I think it's time we thought about your department's future, seriously. For you, as well as the observatory. This isn't good for anyone. You need a break."

"I – just need longer..."

I glance at my computer, but it's asleep. My fists tighten, but I concede. They're right – what's the point, now?

"Take a few days to put your things in order, and we'll get a clean-up crew in to help. Don't worry, we'll take care of you – you've done us all proud, but it's time to stop."

I nod.

"Take the day off, it's nice out." They walk to the exit and open the door, sunlight flooding in as they descend the stairs.

Perhaps I should take their advice. It's probably what you would have recommended too, if you could. I pour a cold mug of coffee and gulp it back, waking my computer.

```
LOADING messages: 2557
Please wait...
```

I choke on coffee, the mug clattering on the floor. This can't be right, can it? I load the first message:

```
1 / 2557
```

```
Sorry this one's so long, I'm certain it won't
come through until we finish the bridge, but I wanted
to get my feelings down before I forget them. I feel
a little stupid writing to nobody, but maybe one day
you'll read all of these. It's been almost a week
since the ban now, and my Head of Department's been
```

replaced. Noone really knows what's happening. And maybe we'll laugh at what a cheesy idiot I'm being, but… I wish you were here, or I was there with you. I know you like your space, but even this is a bit much, right? So we have to make sure we don't lose each other. I'll be thinking of you every day. XXX

There are thousands of messages. *Thousands.* I slide through them desperately, see flashes of letters and memories, pictures and poems, as I near the end – your most recent message: sent today, just 30 minutes ago.

I fall back into my chair, breathless, hot, and open the message:

2557 / 2557

I'm okay. Sorry! You must be worried, but I'm fine, I swear. Better, actually. You realise it now, right? I finished the bridge. Details to follow, but respond ASAP, so I know it works. We have to be quick. XXX

I fumble as I try to type, my hands shaking. I might throw up, but I type:

I GOT IT I FUCKING GOT IT I AM HERE NOW!!! XXX

I wait for a small eternity, and your message arrives. Maybe I'm hallucinating, but I don't care. I open your message:

You: YES! Where's your ID?

Me: here

You: turn it on.

***

our fingers lock, we look out

***

I don't know what you did, or if this is even real, but I obey. I flick the switches and turn on the ID, but its familiar red light flickers. I look back and forth between the ID and my computer, waiting.

```
You: is it on?
Me: yes. What now?
You: wait for green, then initiate
Me: are you kidding?
You: no. are you ready? This might not work.
Me: Yes Yes Yes
YOU: :) I love you.
```

The ID light turns green. I initiate.

Not everything is lost in a failed flight.
Our fingers lock, we look out and wonder
what other worlds there might be. We reminisce
through photographs, see the sun
in each other's eyes, spot words in the stars.
We stretch our arms out, make telescopes
and for a moment, in disbelief, we see.

Catherine Heymans is a Professor of Astrophysics at the University of Edinburgh, Director of the German GCCL Institute and a European Research Council Fellow. She specialises in observing the dark side of our Universe to test whether we need to go beyond Einstein with our current theory of gravity.

The Multiverse

Catherine Heymans

Almost everything that astronomers observe in the Universe can be understood through Einstein's Law of General Relativity. It explains the connectivity between gravity, space, time, energy and matter with a profound conclusion that absolutely nothing can travel faster than 186,000 miles per second, the speed of light. Travelling at this speed you could reach Australia from Scotland in under a tenth of a second, although unfortunately it is predicted that you would gain an infinite amount of mass along the way. Future generations of Earth-born space travellers searching for rapid transportation to a new planet would therefore have to endure serious obesity and a minimum of 4.2 years travelling at light speed to our nearest star Proxima Centauri. To venture outwith our Milky Way galaxy would take even longer, with a minimum 2.5 million year journey to our nearest neighbour, the Andromeda Galaxy.

General Relativity is the best tested theory in Physics, accurately predicting how planets, light rays and satellites move within our own solar system. The next time you navigate a new city with GPS, you can thank Einstein – without an understanding of General Relativity, SatNavs simply wouldn't work. But before we resign ourselves and future space travellers to the limitations that General Relativity imposes upon us, we should note there is one observation of the Universe that Einstein's theory cannot explain.

Our understanding of the Universe is built from a theory that proposes our Universe started with a "Big Bang" 13.8 billion years ago – a small, incredibly hot and dense fiery ball that expanded to create the vast Universe that we see today. Using the same physics that can predict the original temperature of your cup of tea 13.8 minutes after you brewed it, we can predict the temperature of the Universe 13.8 billion years after it was created. Whilst your cooling tea will be emitting infra-red light, the Universe has cooled for so long now it emits low-energy microwave light.

Some readers may be old enough to remember the pre-digital era of television when the screen would show static if it were not tuned to the correct frequency. That static was the detection of low-temperature microwave light, the cooled leftover heat from the Big Bang. Interestingly we find that the vacuum of space across the Universe is exactly and precisely the same low temperature everywhere we look, in every direction across the sky. And it is this observation that is incredibly challenging for a Physicist to explain with only the book of General Relativity in their handbag.

To explain why this is so challenging, I'd invite you to imagine organising a party for one hundred people who have never met each other. You've told them to stop by around 7pm, but they all arrive at 19:13:13 wearing mauve. You either conclude that a highly unlikely cosmic fluke has occurred or that your friends have somehow got connected on Facebook to organise a splendid surprise for your party. Scanning around the Universe today, we see that everywhere we look the Universe is "wearing mauve" (sitting at a temperature of minus 270.4 degrees Celsius precisely). This means that at some point in the past all the different parts of the Universe that we can see today must have been connected, passing on the information that mauve will become the fashionistas' colour for today.

If you are happy with the idea that humanity exists at the very epicentre of the Big Bang and hence the centre of the Universe, then our puzzle is solved. Track back 13.8 billion years, and the Universe that we observe today would have to have been a small but completely connected pea-sized ball, with the current position of the Earth at the very centre of this baby Universe. If, however, you are uncomfortable with the notion that humanity has by some fluke landed in this very special place in the Universe, and you'd like to leave open the possibility that the Universe continues beyond the Horizon, the furthest reaches that we can see, then you have a conundrum. Our General Relativity handbook tells us that nothing can travel faster than the speed of light. The distant Universe that we see on the Northern Horizon is separated by 27.6 billion light years from the distant Universe that we see on the Southern Horizon. Yet somehow in less than 13.8 billion years these two remote regions have worked out how to perfectly mimic each other. Cosmic coincidence? Or is there more to the physics of the Universe than General Relativity alone would predict?

To explain this cosmic conundrum, we need to draw the Inflation Drive (ID) out of our Physicist's handbag. Inflation at this point in time is only a theory, but it is a widely accepted cornerstone theory in our understanding for how the Universe began. This theory proposes that after the Big Bang our pea-sized Universe experienced an essentially instantaneous period of rapid expansion at a rate *faster than the speed of light*. In the first moments in the hot dense environment of our embryonic Universe, the four fundamental forces are thought to have worked as one unified force, imparting a staggering amount of energy to the Universe to inflate it to the cosmic scales that we see today.

Take yourself back to your youth, sitting at the top of a hill with your toy car sat stationary next to you. You don't touch it and are simply enjoying the view. Very slowly your car will start to edge down the slope, picking up speed along the way until it is racing down the hill at rapid speed. Your toddler self will marvel as there are no batteries and you didn't push the car – instead it is the force of gravity that has donated its energy to move your toy car down the hill. In the same way, the unified forces can donate energy to expand the post Big-Bang Universe at rapid speeds, faster than light itself.

This theory of inflation solves our Horizon conundrum by

allowing previously connected regions of our Universe to now be separated by distances further than light can travel throughout the history of the Universe. It also allows us to conceive the possibility for future faster-than-light travel. It has a potentially nasty side-effect though that future space travellers must heed. Much like a toy car rolling down a hill requires a force to stop it, the Inflation Drive causes an expansion so vast and immediate that a huge force must be imparted for the inflation to cease. For our toy car, the hill may simply flatten and friction will slow our car to a halt, or our car may crash into a wall. For our Universe it is hard to derive methods to halt the inflation once it has started. There are several theories on the possible outcome of stopping the drive, including the creation of alternate universes which co-exist with our own. In these "chaotic" theories, for every single universe created by Inflation, another two or more universes are created when the initial period of inflation halts. Chaotic inflationary models are not fictional and can and are being tested by looking for subtle patterns in the microwave relic radiation from the Inflationary era. If observations support these chaotic theories, we will have to conclude that our Universe is not alone and is one in a sea of many universes within the Multiverse.

Matjaz Vidmar is a researcher in Science, Technology and Innovation
Studies at the University of Edinburgh. He is an (Astro)Physicist by training,
now examining innovation and organisational change as well as other
social dimensions of Astronomy and Outer Space Exploration and Industry.
You can find more at www.roe.ac.uk/~vidmar

Of Maps, Love Stories
and the Universe

Matjaz Vidmar

Natural sciences, in particular Physics and Astrophysics, are organised around the core premise of trying to identify, characterise and interlink our understandings of the "laws of nature". These laws can perhaps best be described as defined permanent links between past, present and future states of matter. Imagine the intermesh of these established links as a kind of map, plotting out a landscape of how our Universe works, even though we can never really see the hills and rivers and seas that scientists try to describe. This scientific topography of our experience of the world is an attempt to abstractly represent the restrictions placed on us by physical reality.

However, any map is a reflection on its maker, reflecting their interests and disinterests. We make travel maps to tell us about accessible roads and to avoid obstacles such as high cliffs; we care about our destinations and the landmarks that will lead us to them. Such maps do not plot out all the individual trees in the forest, record the smell of meadows, or show lines to represent the flight-paths of birds. Needless to say, that does not mean they do not as accurately as possible describe the landscape to which they correspond. It is unlikely a map will show a hill summit where there is not one, but if the cartographer is not interested in hills, they may choose to omit hills altogether from their plot. Maps are thus very "political" artefacts – they are made with a purpose and reflect the priorities of their makers.

Any scientific mapping of our Universe, then, can be understood as prioritising certain aspects of our understanding over others, based on societal interests. This is sometimes referred to as relativism – that if science is a product of social life, then its achievements are relative to the society producing it. Such a constructivist understanding of science as a system does not disagree with the notion that natural systems impose constraints on scientific knowledge-making; rather, it describes any such work as a product of societal attempts to apply order to the natural world, and not solely "discover" it.

These activities to scientifically map the Universe link physical reality with interpretive narration of our individual and collective experiences: we form stories about the "landscape" we inhabit. This is often achieved by establishing some narrative structure to link the inner, individual, cognitive perception with the outer, collective, contextual experience of our existence. In this sense, a scientific "story" is both a mechanism of sense-making within the Universe's landscape as well as a narrative device to add or extract specific information to and from our mapping of it. Thus, we can understand stories as explorations of maps, and maps as congregated, structured and interrelated stories.

Critically, for any story to work successfully, it has to enrol its audience in a shared recognition of which map we are drawing up or reading and which interests are at stake in it. Narrative devices can be used for establishing such communally shared recognition and linking our experience of the world around us to those of others and, finally, the overarching topology of our Universe. It seems that creating harmonious order and structure in the face of randomness and chaos is a guiding principle behind constructing these stories and maps that link them together. In symmetry, disorganised and dissonant narratives are not so much contrary to these concepts as they are their opposing manifestation. However, for any such structure to work, its audience has to agree on what harmonious and dissonant narratives look like, and, critically, under which rules these can be established, maintained or broken. For instance, the narrative form for most of these stories, scientific and artistic, tends to be cyclical. They start from a stable state of existence that is perturbed by some existential struggle to retain or expand the map we created of the landscape.

Catherine's essay provides an example of this from science. The theory of cosmic inflation, or the Inflation Drive, has been proposed in order to explain the faster than light (in fact, near instantaneous) expansion of the Universe in its very early moments. A massive amount of energy was needed to start this expansion, and an equal and opposite amount of energy would have been required to stop it, something which should not be possible due to one of the core Physics principles called "conservation of energy of an isolated system", i.e. no new energy can be created within the Universe if it is not already there. But here is the twist in this story: the theory side-steps this issue by proposing that the Inflation Drive might have been stopped by creating parallel universe(s), from which the energy to stop the expansion was drawn. The consequent total system now becomes a Multiverse, and the total energy of this new (bigger) isolated system is preserved.

Of couse, storytelling is not by any means limited to science; fictional literary stories map out a landscape of shared understanding in a similar way. We can look to Russell's story of star-struck lovers, separated through physical and social forces, who strive to come together through reconnecting the maps of their physical and social landscapes. Importantly, their personal perspectives and motivations are also reflections of their collective's visions and trends. By adding, extracting and configuring our common maps of physical and societal landscapes, we define not only who we are as individuals but what we are as a community or society. Furthermore, it is often the case that as much as we may try to attain independence and expand autonomy from others, our interconnectedness and dependence is subsequently reinstated through the resulting redefinition of the "other" – in the case of the scientists in Russell's story, the others are firstly defined as a different country, then the (political) controllers who have broken the shared maps and travel mechanisms, and finally the scientific friends and colleagues who believe the maps cannot be mended. The "other" is always there as we seek to establish our own identity against it.

This pervasive narrative form of re-defining the other, which is found in both Catherine's and Russell's pieces, illuminates a fundamental principle of our storytelling and cartography, and perhaps our existence as a whole: that wherever and whatever we look at, we have far more in common than that which divides us. As noted earlier, there is a symmetry in these stories, as any design to achieve independence from this commonality is at its core yet another manifestation of our collective togetherness. In the realisation of the commonality of our interrelatedness, we can perhaps also better appreciate the similarities between the activities of a scientist and an artist, between a factual story and an invented one. Narrative creation of stories to make sense of the world, and continuously expanding them with new ideas and information, leads to an ever-expanding communal mapping of our Universe.

In a flight of fancy, one could perhaps even go as far as propose that there are features in the Universe itself which force us towards these kinds of storytelling and mapping activities. For example, a quite prominent landmark in our scientific mapping of the Universe is a principle which Physicists refer to as the second law of thermodynamics. Loosely interpreted, it states that in all natural systems energy irreversibly dissipates in order to average out towards the minimum total equilibrium, i.e. until all available space is filled with the same amount of energy. In a famous example, heat always naturally flows from hot to cold bodies and never in the reverse. This dissipation of energy also leads to an increase of entropy (the amount of disorder in the system), since energy is minimised when ordered structures are broken apart.

Due to the Universe's continuous spatial expansion, the amount of structured energy at any given spot is continuously decreasing. As proposed in one of the leading theories of cosmological evolution, the Universe is thus doomed to eventually stretch out so much that all matter will lose its structure and the Universe's global temperature will come down to very close to absolute zero – something referred to as the Heat Death. Hence, our best understanding of the Universe's life-span describes a cycle, too; having emerged from free-moving fundamental particles with high energy and in a small space, the Universe struggled to form landscape structures and retain them, but will return back to free-moving fundamental particles once all the energy is averaged out to an infinitesimal fraction above absolute zero. The continuous increase of entropy is thus linked to how we understand the cosmological passage of time.

However, this entropic dissipation of energy is met with what appears to be local "entropic resistance". Linkages within matter provide resistance to entropy by structuring energy. Examples include quantum and nuclear bonds between sub-atomic particles, and chemical bonds between atoms to form molecules. Some energy is permanently stored in those bonds and they require additional energy to break them. Information can be treated as a type of bonding energy as well, as it is a key linking block between particles of matter. In miniscule quantum phenomena, information about states of matter leads to changes to those states – for instance knowing a particle's physical quantity (e.g. spin) leads to a specific response from the system (e.g. there becomes a particle with an opposite spin). Due to the physical effects of these bonds, some energy must be stored in them, and hence creation of information can lead to structuring and retaining energy.

Building up from the quantum scale, these energy-structuring phenomena are at the basis of the most complex physical systems, such as humans and our physical and social interlinking. Through this, the curious map we are making gets yet another layer: our interaction with the Universe's landscapes, by creating stories and mapping them together, can be seen as a form of entropic resistance in itself. One could argue that embedding this entropic resistance into its landscape is the Universe's response to its own doom. Through structural ordering of matter and information, the natural systems retain as much energy for as long as possible and, hence, slow down the rate of entropic decay. In a way, our collective love for creating information through storytelling and mapping could be a result of the Universe's self-referential love for its own existence.

However, this is only yet another story. Is it drawn from the purely fictional layer of the map we have been drafting, or does it feature in the physical reality of the Universe's landscape, too? Perhaps it can at least serve as an illustration of the point made earlier, that whilst our approaches might be different, whether through science, art or other means, our sense-making is tightly and critically based around stories interlinked and merged into maps, plotting a shared experience of the landscape we inhabit. Hence, it should not be too surprising that the resulting map may well feature landmarks implying that the narratives we bring into existence are both the manifestations of our relational interdependence, as well as expressions of love for (and from) the Universe itself.

Colin McInnes is James Watt Chair, Professor of Engineering Science at the University of Glasgow. His research interests include spacecraft orbital dynamics, solar sailing, space resources and other advanced space concepts.

His work is currently supported by a Royal Academy of Engineering Chair in Emerging Technologies.

Afterword

Colin R McInnes

For a small nation, Scotland has given much to the world of science and engineering. While many are familiar with the names of Kelvin, Maxwell and Watt, the visionary thinking of William Leitch is perhaps less well known. A minister from Rothesay who studied Mathematics at the University of Glasgow, Leitch apparently provided the earliest scientific description of rocket propulsion for spaceflight. Writing in 1861, Leitch noted that by relying on Newton's third law of motion, rocket propulsion would be effective in a vacuum. This was many years before the writing of the better-known pioneers, such as Goddard and Tsiolkovsky. In a rather odd historical oversight, it is believed that Leitch's work went largely unnoticed since his books were catalogued under theology, rather than the natural sciences.

With such a visionary, although little-known past, it's therefore fitting that Scotland should now have a central role in the development of modern space technology. Through various commercial ventures it's said that Glasgow now manufactures more spacecraft than any other European city. Small spacecraft, to be clear, but that's the point of the so-called 'New Space' movement. Combined with the prospect of local 'spaceports' for small satellite launches, Scotland has found itself to be a key space-faring nation here in the early years of the 21st century.

Looking to the future, perhaps Scotland can offer the world more than science and engineering for the 21st century. The Apollo-era astronauts from half a century ago often expressed their sense of transcendence in viewing the Earth from deep space, but all too quickly the next item on their check-list called for attention. But even modern scientific missions using robotic spacecraft are still very much human-centred endeavours. The machines themselves are merely projections of our senses, imprinted on silicon, and launched into the darkness. While many of us are moved in a quite visceral way by new images of other worlds, few can truly articulate their deeper meaning to us as Earth-bound explorers. Perhaps through Scotland's pioneering work on the small spacecraft of the future, rather than the giants of Apollo from the past, we can provide a deeper sense of meaning than is offered at present.

Importantly, while space exploration is often seen as a venture for science and engineering, it is essential that this very human-centred endeavour be reflected and critiqued through the arts, as has been done so ably in this book. Through the arts, we can surely better understand our journeys of exploration. In particular, through the imagination of science fiction, we can critique our motivations for entering space and anticipate how new space technologies will shape our common future. Such critiques need not be directed only at outward facing trips to the moon or Mars. We can reflect on the impact of the growing constellation of satellites pointing inwards which view the entire Earth system from space; its environment, people and economy. Perhaps Scotland's contribution will be to provide entirely new vantage points, both technological and philosophical, from which to better understand the sheer richness of life on Earth.

About Shoreline of Infinity

Shoreline of Infinity is a science fiction and fantasy focused publisher and events host based in Edinburgh, Scotland.

As well as a range of science fiction related publications Shoreline of Infinity also publishes a quarterly science fiction magazine featuring new short stories, poetry, artwork, reviews and articles.

Writers we've published include: Iain M. Banks, Jane Yolen, Nalo Hopkison, Charles Stross, Eric Brown, Ken MacLeod, Ada Palmer, Gary Gibson, Jeannette Ng, Adam Roberts, Jo Walton, Bo Bolander, Tim Majors. We're equally proud of all the new writers we've published.

Shoreline of Infinity Science Fiction Magazine received British Fantasy Society Award 2018 for best magazine/periodical.

Shoreline of Infinity also hosts Event Horizon – a monthly live science fiction cabaret in Edinburgh.

To find out more, visit the website:

www.shorelineofinfinity.com

and follow us on Twitter: @shoreinf

Lightning Source UK Ltd.
Milton Keynes UK
UKHW020734171119
353697UK00006B/51/P